MW00477989

This book is a work of fiction.
product of the author's imagin
to any person, living or dead is

Summary: Wayne, a bully at his previous school, spends the summer reinventing himself. Two of his summer reads end up making a tremendous impact on him. When the school year begins, Wayne is resolved to no longer be a bully at his new school. On the very first day, he unwittingly gets caught up in a school shooting. Faced with the prospect of being found by one of the shooters, Wayne uses the skills he had learned over the summer to take the shooters down. In the aftermath of the school shooting, Wayne finds himself caught up in an intense and very interesting discussion with his peers regarding children becoming school shooters. They talk about guns, gun control, mental health diagnosis as well as therapies, the state of our educational system, and potential solutions and measures to prevent school shootings, and hopefully, all mass shootings. Although the discussion veers into uncertain territory, everyone is agreed about one thing – something has to change.

Testimonial from **Dr. Scott Poland, National School Violence Responder and Prevention Trainer** – "A timely masterpiece as we all search for solutions to school violence. This book is a must read for educators, parents, and students in today's world." **Dr. Poland was a first responder at the Columbine High School shooting in 1999.**

ISBN: 9781695259621
This book was typeset in Goudy Old Style.

Visit us at drmayi.com to learn about other book projects. Please review this book on goodreads.com. To leave reviews on Amazon, you have to sign into your amazon account. To read about Wayne during his bullying days, visit amazon.com to get a copy of the book 'Mrs. A' by Bindu Mayi.

In memory of my parents, my pillars of love and kindness.

SOMETHING HAS TO CHANGE

TABLE OF CONTENT

	Chapter	Page Number
1	CHANGE IS IN THE AIR	1 – 6
2	INCONSEQUENTIAL	7 – 15
3	MORRIE	16 – 27
4	DARTS	28 – 37
5	GUNS	38 – 53
6	NOBEL PRIZE WINNERS	54 – 61
7	SOCIAL STUDIES	62 – 69
8	OCD	70 – 80
9	A HERO	81 – 94
10	THE AFTERMATH	95 – 103
11	NOT ONE MORE SCHOOL	104 – 124
12	SOMETHING HAS TO CHANGE	125 – 135
13	SOLUTIONS	136 – 155
14	THE MARSHMALLOW	156 – 169
Request to you		170
Acknowledgments		171
About the Author		172
Note from the Author		173 – 174

CHAPTER 1
CHANGE IS IN THE AIR

"Don't shoot. Please don't shoot. Please. I'm innocent. Help me. Please." I had my hands up in the air and I was screaming at the top of my voice. I was frantically trying to convince the police that I was innocent. I didn't even know if they could hear me.

Everyone was shouting at once. And then, my body did this thing where I could see myself from the outside. I had thrown myself on the floor and was laying there, not moving, hands on my head. Oh shit! I was dead at just 14 years, I thought, thinking back to other people who had out-of-body experiences as they lay dying. Soon, there was a swarm of uniformed officers around me.

How did I get to this all-time low of feeling hunted? Like a wild animal! To get to this point, let me take you to an earlier memory of the time when I was 13. I had been rushed to the hospital with what turned out to be a MRSA infection.

My first recollection of my hospital stay is of the nurse saying, "Well, that was a nasty infection there, young man. If it weren't for your mother, I don't know. You are so lucky." She changed the bag on my IV pole, patted me on the head, and said, "You probably got an insect bite on your leg and scratched it, which then got infected."

Mom spoke up at this point and said, "Nope. A kid in school stabbed him with a pencil."

"Whoa, really?! Sounds like a lawsuit," said the nurse.

Mom's eyes lit up at that, and she looked at me and smiled.

I closed my eyes. I didn't want to argue with my mom. I knew the truth. The kid she was talking about was Andy, and he hadn't stabbed me with that pencil. I had tried to stab him, and he had only defended himself. So when he pushed away, I pushed back hard and ended up stabbing myself in the leg. There you have it. **That's** the pure truth. But Mom was so enthralled with her version of the story, I did not dare remind her of the truth.

"Stay in bed and rest, young man," said the nurse, as she was leaving the room.

I kept my eyes closed. I could feel my mom ruffling my hair and straightening my sheets. She then kissed me and said, "I am right here, love. Right here on this chair."

I drifted in and out of consciousness, and pretty soon, I started dreaming.

"Where's Mommy today? Why did you come to get me, Marcy?"
There was fear in the little boy's voice, although he tried hard to keep all emotion from his face.

Marcy said nothing. She just took Regis's hand in her own and started walking.

Regis was four and his sister, Marcy, was 18. All day in preschool, he had thought of his mom. She hadn't been in the kitchen cooking him breakfast that morning. And that always meant one thing and one thing only. Dad was home and was in her room.

"Dear God, please don't let him hurt her this time. Please, dear God, please." Instead of singing along with his teacher and the other kids in preschool, he was so busy praying, he did not notice his friend, Alice, looking at him with concern.

Alice lived across the street from Regis, and she had heard her mom talk to her dad about Dr. Martin, Regis's dad. Alice's mom thought Regis's dad beat Regis's mom from time to time, but there was nothing she could do to help. It didn't help that Mrs. Martin never talked to her or to any of the neighbors. But Alice's mom always made sure that Alice was nice to Regis. Sometimes, she even packed lunch for Regis.

While Regis was in school, his sister, Marcy, was at work. She had started work right after high school. She did not want to be like her mother and depend on a man for everything. "Ouch, watch it, Regis." Regis had squeezed his sister's hand pretty hard as he thought about his parents. He was terrified of getting home and finding that their dad had hurt their mom, again.

"Stop it, Regis, you are squeezing my hand too tight."

"I am sorry, Marcy."

Brother and sister were both thinking the same thoughts, but did not dare voice them. Once they did, they could never pretend that everything was fine. They could no longer pretend that their dad loved them just like his friends thought he did. When his friends from work came over, their dad would make Regis, Marcy, and their mom wear their best clothes. He would have Regis hang onto his arms or sit on his lap, while he made everyone laugh with his never-ending stories about his patients. The times they had guests over for a huge feast, were getting fewer and fewer.

Marcy put the key in the door, and as soon as she opened the door, Regis was in the house and rushing up the stairs, to look for his mom. He knew not to yell out for her. He knew there were times when she was in so much pain that even his whispers hurt her head.

He ran into her room, his heart pounding, and had to stuff his fist into his mouth to stop his moan of anguish and fear.

His mom lay on the bed, her right eye swollen shut. Regis rushed to her and then rushed back to close the door. He was terrified that his dad might still be around. But Marcy pushed her way in before he had a chance to lock the door.

Marcy's hands clenched and her face scrunched up in pain and anger. "I am going to pay him a call in his clinic."

She looked at Regis and said, "Stay here with her. Do you know how to freshen her up?"

Regis nodded. He had seen Marcy clean their mother up scores of times. Without a word, he went into the bathroom, and trying not

4

to make too much noise, he got a washcloth, wet it with hot water, tiptoed to his mom, and set about wiping her face. She wept silently, her tears making his hands shake.

Regis went into the bathroom again and started filling up the tub with hot water. He dumped in some Epsom salts and her favorite essential oils, rose and jasmine. He went back in, and sweeping his mom's beautiful black hair away from her face, he said, "Mom, your bath is ready. I am outside the door. Please call me if you need anything."

Regis took out two towels and kept them by the tub before leaving the room. He knew Marcy would be home later that night. And he prayed that his dad wouldn't be home for at least a few days.

Later that night, Regis and his mom had just finished their peanut butter and jelly sandwiches when there was a loud knock on the door. The two looked at each other. Regis knew it couldn't be Marcy or his dad, as they both had a key to the house.

Mother and son walked to the door and Regis opened it. It was a policeman.

When he saw Regis's mom, he took off his cap, and without quite looking at her, he said, "Ma'am, I am afraid there's been an accident."

Regis looked over at his mom and saw the desperation as well as hope in her eyes before she closed them and asked, "Who?"

The cop cleared his throat and said, "Your husband."

Regis caught the brilliance of his mother's smile and then he would never ever forget the next few seconds of his life.

"And your daughter, Marcy. I am afraid they are both dead."

Regis heard a crash and looked down. His mother had slumped to the floor, unconscious.

When I woke up from that horrible dream, I was drenched in sweat. I looked over at Mom and she was slouched in her chair, fast asleep.

I remembered everything now. That was not a bad dream – that was the memory of my childhood. My name used to be Regis. My mom must've changed it at some point to remove all associations with my dad, whose middle name was Regis.

I didn't know much about domestic abuse. But I knew now that my mom had been battered and abused. I didn't know why I had suppressed those earlier days of my life, back when I was Regis. Remembering such an oppressed part of my life made me feel angry and frustrated. My mind was racing with questions I had no way of answering. Why would these memories come up now? What good could they do? How was I supposed to work through them? Did I really need to work through them? Was I a bully because I had witnessed physical abuse first hand?

Soon, I would get answers to many of these questions.

CHAPTER 2
INCONSEQUENTIAL

I was out of the hospital and back in school, even though there were only a few weeks left for the end of the school year. I knew there wouldn't be any fanfare, but I was not prepared for the hostility.

"Hey, why are you back?" I heard that all day, but I said nothing as per our lawyer's instructions.

Mom had hired a lawyer to sue the school as well as the boy who "gave me" MRSA. Mom said we could get so much money that she would never need to work again.

I hadn't been privy to all of the conversations between Mom and the lawyer, but the whole lawsuit was based on a small, white lie.

Mom was animated by the idea that Andy had stabbed me with a pencil and that wound was what gave me the horrible MRSA infection.

I would never, no matter how many lies I would have to tell, say something to ruin Mom's day. Mom would smile every time she thought of suing the school, and so, the white lie stayed.

When the lawyer asked me if Andy had stabbed me, I said "Yes," in a clear, loud voice.

After almost three weeks since my last day at school, I walked back in the front doors. Yes, there were whispers. I heard Andy's name quite a few times.

I walked into my classroom and sat far away from the spot where Andy had stabbed me. I mean, I knew he hadn't stabbed me, but I had almost convinced myself that he had. There was no way I was letting anyone know that if Andy had let me stab him, he would have been the one getting stabbed and not me!

Aaron, the only kid in class who was bigger than me, shouted out, "Hey Wayne, are you going to thank Andy for saving your life?"

What the heck, I thought to myself. Was this some kind of a sick joke they thought they could play on me, once I was back? Why the heck would Andy save my life? I knew how much I had tortured him all these years. He would never, not in a million years, do anything to help me, let alone save my life. I knew I wouldn't, if our roles had been reversed.

Mrs. Wilson, the math teacher, came in just then, and the class became quiet. But instead of starting her class, she walked towards Andy and said, "Son, Mr. Campbell would like to speak with you."

She then walked towards me and said, "You too, Wayne. Principal's office, now."

The class started whispering and talking all at once.

When we got to the Principal's office, Mom was there. Her face was red and she looked angry. Her lawyer was with her, and he looked angry too.

I was excited. I wanted Mom to win this lawsuit. The school had never been nice to me. Well, alright, I did bully some of the kids, but then none of them had ever been nice to me. They always ignored me. Why the heck would I be nice to them? I wanted each and every single one of them to feel the pain of being ignored. I knew they laughed at me behind my back. I knew they thought me so inconsequential, they felt they could get away with not being friends with me.

I went over to Mom and sat next to her.

Mr. Campbell, the Principal, looked worried. Good, I thought. I had no respect for him. He had never scolded me for bullying other kids.

I knew what I was doing was wrong, but I really couldn't help it. That was the only way I could get rid of the overwhelming fury and sorrow that was inside me.

Besides, when I looked at some of the kids, all I could remember was how mean they were to me and how they never acknowledged me. The next thing I knew, I was either tripping them as they walked by or elbowing them hard. It felt good, especially when I could hear them grunt in pain. I was happy to hurt them first. I knew that if they were scared of me, they would not hurt me.

Mr. Campbell gestured to a chair and said to Andy, "Sit down, son. Tell us what you know about Wayne's pencil stab."

I looked at Andy out of the corner of my eye and I was surprised to see him sitting up straight. I remembered Andy as a kid who slouched, and always looked dirty, and never made eye contact. He didn't look dirty now, and he was looking Mr. Campbell in the eye.

I heard Andy say, "I was in class when I saw something come towards me. It was Wayne, and he had a pencil in his hand. He was trying to stab me. But I caught his hand and deflected it away from me. When he tried to move closer towards me to forcefully stab me, he ended up stabbing himself in the leg."

Mr. Campbell removed his glasses and rubbed his eyes. Putting his glasses back on, he looked at Andy and said, "Thank you, Andy." He then looked at me and said, "Will you give us your version of the story, Wayne?"

I looked at Mom and when she nodded at me, I prepared myself to lie again. I looked down at my leg, reminding myself of the ordeal that Andy had put us through and said, "Andy stabbed me with his pencil. I did not try to stab him. He stabbed me."

Andy was shaking his head.

"Don't you dare shake your head! Who do you think you are? You gave my son MRSA and I have a lawyer here who will take you and your school to court. You stabbed my boy, Wayne. And you" Mom turned to point at Mr. Campbell while glaring at him, "had a dirty enough school that gave him MRSA. I will sue your school."

I was really scared now, thinking to myself, "What will happen if they find out I was lying?"

"Mr. Campbell, sir," I heard Andy speak up. "I would like to make a phone call. Please."

Mr. Campbell asked, "Who are you trying to call, son?"

"If I am being sued, I would like to have my own lawyer here to represent me." Andy's tone was low. He sounded scared.

Mr. Campbell nodded and handed the phone to Andy.

While Andy was speaking softly into the phone so that none of us could hear him, I pulled up my pant leg and looked at the scar on my leg. It still looked angry, like a battle wound meant to always remind me of something. Except in this case, all I could remember was no one at school had said *Welcome back, we missed you.*

Finally, Andy asked, "Mr. Campbell, did they test to see if they could pick up MRSA from any of the school locker rooms or equipment they cleaned?"

Mr. Campbell shook his head. "They just cleaned. They didn't test any of it."

Andy was back on the phone some more before hanging up. "Mr. Campbell, if it is alright with you, I would like to get back to class. We are doing trigonometry."

Mr. Campbell nodded at Andy and said, "I am proud of you, son."

Andy was almost at the door when I heard him say, "I am glad you recovered, Wayne."

I heard a snort and looked up at Mom. She was muttering something under her breath, looking red faced and angry.

I could see Andy standing at the door and he must have been looking at me. I didn't have the desire or courage to look at him.

Neither Mom nor I acknowledged Andy's remark, but our lawyer looked surprised, and then embarrassed.

When Andy left, Mom decided that I didn't need to stay in school, and I left with her and our lawyer.

But we were back at school the next day. When we got there, we met with one of the county doctors whose task it was to investigate the origins of my MRSA infection. He stuck what looked like fancy Q tips up our noses, and then put them in special tubes. He said he would know the result in two days.

I didn't stay in school that day. On the way home, Mom asked me if I would like to go to a new school. I said, I would love to.

I was sick of everyone calling Andy a hero. I just couldn't stomach the fact that he didn't seem to be a loser anymore. How did he do that? How does a person go from zero to hero? Beats me! All of a sudden, everyone seemed to really like him and look up to him. I didn't care for that at all.

When we got home, Mom sat me down and said, "Wayne, I want you to know I am getting married again."

I shrugged. I mean, what could I say? I knew she was seeing her accountant, Eugene. It was the happiest I had ever seen my mom. Personally, I didn't think we needed anyone. And I thought, I was the man of the house.

I asked, "Is it Eugene, Mom? Do I need to give him my permission?"

She laughed at that and said, "Yes, love, it's Eugene. He loves me very much." She took my hand in hers and continued, "He has asked us to move in with him. That means a new school district and a new school."

I smiled. It was my first smile of the day.

It would be nice to not go back to my old school. A hellhole. I got angry every single time I walked up the steps to my school.

Two glorious days of not going to school and then we had to go back. Our lawyer picked us up in his new Maserati Gran Turismo.

We were the first ones to get to Mr. Campbell's office. As soon as we got settled in, Andy's lawyer walked in, followed soon by Dr. Schreir, the doctor who was responsible for figuring out where my MRSA infection came from.

Long story short, you will never ever believe where that MRSA came from. It came from my mom. She was livid. She grabbed my hand and we almost ran out of there.

In the car ride back home, the only sound was the thrumming of our lawyer's car and the occasional roar when he put it in Sport mode.

Since the lawyer was Mom's boyfriend's best friend, he didn't charge us a dime. We didn't owe him anything.

When Mom finally spoke up, it was to say defiantly, "Even if I gave my son MRSA, Andy still stabbed him. It was THAT stab that gave MRSA an entryway into the body. I still want to sue him."

Our lawyer didn't say anything. When the car finally stopped at a light, he looked over at me for a long time – well, at least until the car behind us honked at him to go. I think he suspected there was more to Andy's story than I was letting on.

Clearing his throat, he looked at my mom and said, "I don't recommend any more threats or lawsuits. Andy comes from a very poor household. If you sue him, you won't get anything there. And I don't recommend suing the school. They will say that it was a lack of good hand hygiene that allowed MRSA entry into Wayne's wound. And that puts the culpability on you both."

Mom started saying something, but the lawyer spoke over her and said, "I spoke to Eugene and he said to walk away. You are changing schools anyway."

School was almost over for the year, so I didn't go back at all. I had enough shame in me to know there was no way I could be around Andy. I had heard enough whispers to know that it was at his insistence that my Mom had called 911. The ambulance had rushed me to the hospital and I had received treatment for a really bad, MRSA infection. For the life of me, I could not fathom why Andy would try to save my life. I had taken great pleasure in tormenting him. I wondered if he was one of those religious people who thought everyone was made in God's image. If so, what did he think of Hitler? Or any of our serial killers?!

Mom had to go to a doctor to get treated for carrying MRSA bacteria in her nose.

CHAPTER 3
MORRIE

Mom got married that summer. We moved into a new house in a new school district. The house was enormous! I realized I could go for hours without seeing anybody. We even had a housekeeper, Martha.

I did a lot of thinking and growing up that summer. Being hospitalized with a potentially deadly infection had something to do with it, for sure. I had nothing else to do but think, the entire time I was in the hospital.

I was also really curious about how Andy had brought about his transformation. He had been such a dud. No friends, no skills, and no knowledge whatsoever of anything at all. I was thinking, if Andy could go from a nobody to being surrounded by friends and getting the top grades in school, perhaps I could also reinvent myself.

We spent two weeks on a boat, sailing around Southern Italy. Mom's new husband, Eugene, was a lot older than Mom. He got mistaken for my grandfather at times. But he was really rich, which meant he could take entire summers off without having to work. And he was old school, which was another word for *not fond of all the newfangled technology that "saps children's brains."* What exactly did that mean for me? No access to the internet! But we had an entire library of books. Eugene encouraged me to read some of those books.

I didn't like doing what I was told to do. So, the first day I spent all day on the deck, staring out into the Tyrrhenian Sea, pretending there were killer sharks circling our boat.

I was 5 feet, 7 inches tall and according to Mom, still growing. Eugene had said the Tyrrhenian Sea was about 12,000 feet deep. I would have to have about 2,150 of me standing one on top of another, to touch the bottom of that sea.

Oh, yeah. I felt insignificant. For the first time, I also felt a strange calm. I felt the waves pulling away at my anger until all that remained was the rhythm of my breathing, the sound of the waves, and the bobbing of the boat. The water just seemed to keep on moving. If its only purpose was to keep moving and keep flowing, I felt that ships, barges, boats, and all the other man-made, water traffic that hampered the movement of the water was anti-water.

The water seemed to have accepted everything we were doing to it. The oil spills, the traffic, the over-fishing. Very forgiving. Was it the same water from millions or even billions of years ago? Did you have to be old enough to have seen it all to realize that forgiveness means you get to keep on flowing?

I wondered what my flow or movement was supposed to be. Staring into that ancient and ever moving water, I couldn't help but go over everything that had ever happened to me or not happened to me, because of who I was or wasn't. I felt ashamed of some of the things I had said and done.

Remembering how deep the water was helped me realize that my problems were small. I realized there was no reason for me to be attached to who I had been in the past. I could be forgiving of who I used to be. I could reinvent myself going forward. I lost track of time that day, out there on the deck, staring into the ocean.

Unfortunately, the not doing what I was told to do also extended to sunscreen. By the time Mom joined me on the deck, I had already turned red like a lobster.

The sunburn kept me indoors for the remainder of the week. I did not like sleeping during the day, so in the middle of my first day indoors, I made my way to the library.

One of the maids on the yacht was finishing her cleaning, when I entered.

"Hello! Do you like to read?" asked the young, red-headed girl with green eyes and a big smile.

I stared at her, mesmerized by that smile. It lit up her entire face.

I was about to tell her that I hated reading, when I remembered I wanted to reinvent myself.

"Yes," I said. "Do you recommend anything?"

She gave another dazzling smile, turned around and almost skipped to the bookshelf. Pausing for a brief second, she grabbed a book and brought it back to me.

"I just finished reading it and absolutely loved it."

I looked at the cover. It said 'Tuesdays with Morrie'.

I read the acknowledgments first and counted 11 people who had helped the author in creating that book. Eugene said you can count a man's wealth by his friends. The author, Mitch Albom, must be very wealthy, I thought. The complete opposite of me.

The first page immediately grabbed my attention. It had the word death in it. A few pages in, something created such a jolt in me that I re-read it a few times. I would have typed it into my phone, except Mom had put it away. I ran over to the desk, grabbed a notebook and a pen, and came back to my chair.

"Do I wither up and disappear or do I make the best of my time left?" Morrie, the professor, had said this.

There were so many times during the school year that I had wished for exactly that. To disappear. Nothingness held a lot of appeal. Sometimes I would pretend to be a body floating in deep space, with no one around me. That was the only time I felt still, the only time no one could make me feel inadequate or insult me. I wasn't so dumb as to not see the irony in that. I knew I was a bully. I could not help it. I had so much anger inside me. If I didn't hit someone or yell at someone or say something really nasty, I felt I would implode. I felt if I didn't threaten them, they would eat me alive. I bullied to protect myself. I refused to be pitied or hurt. I'd much rather hurt someone than have them hurt me. Hurting me was just not going to happen.

Ever since I had remembered Mom's horrendous abuse at my dad's hands, a small part of me wondered if that was why I had so much anger inside me.

Reading that line in 'Tuesdays with Morrie' was the first time I had seen an alternative to disappearing. Making the best of my time left. What a crazy idea!

I probably had another 60 or 70 years left. It felt exhausting to contemplate even another year of being friendless, especially now that Mom was finally happy.

I wrote in my notebook, "*What if I didn't bully? What if my new persona was like Andy's new persona?*" Andy had metamorphosized from being a zero with no friends and no ambition, to being a hero who had saved my life.

That thought made me so jumpy, I had to get up and walk around a bit before calming down enough to start reading again. A few more pages in and something the author said made me get up and walk around again – something about seeking his identity in toughness and how it was his teacher's softness that drew him in and made him relax.

I wrote down a few more words from the book and scribbled my thoughts next to it:

PURPOSE - *I have no clue what mine is. If I don't have a purpose, does that mean I can be more easily distracted by thoughts and desires of bullying? Maybe, if I have an actual purpose, I won't be so focused on others, but can focus on what it is that I can ~~do create~~ achieve?*

MEANING - *I will pay attention to the meaning behind my actions. If my anger from my past makes me a bully in the present, I really have to forget that anger. I have to forget what created all that anger. Forget, and create better memories.*

COMPASSION - *I have felt this for my mom and no one else, not even me. I will try hard to think more about this.*

HUMAN KINDNESS - *I like how kind Eugene is to Mom and me. It's not really what he says to us, it's how he says it – you can feel the love. I don't know how to do that. Can I just copy Eugene?*

HUMAN - *I will remind myself that I am human, and that I am also, only a young human. I cannot act like a wild animal and lash out, and if I do, I just need to chill. I am young, and still learning.*

FORGIVENESS - *I need to <u>cultivate</u> it. I am so angry, it's hard to forgive anyone. But, after thinking about this word, I realize I need to forgive myself too – for being angry almost all the time.*

EXPERIENCE FULLY - *I want to soak up all the moments because there are people who don't get that chance.*

DETACH - *I am not sure what this means yet, but I will pay attention to my life, so I can figure out when I need to detach and what I need to detach from.*

There was a quote in the book that made me stop and scratch my head a few times – not just that day, but over the next few days, and months. "<u>We don't see what we could be</u>."

It made me think. What do I not see that I could be?
Could I become a smart kid and turn my life around, like Andy? Could I also have friends? Could I be something other than a bully? Could I get rid of my anger? I saw the snide looks other kids gave each other when they saw me. They were smart enough not to say anything to my face. But I couldn't stop them from saying whatever it is that they said behind my back.

A cornered rat. That's what I felt like. Nobody likes rats, except maybe for their mothers.

I wasn't a smart kid. I bullied others. I was angry. Lonely. For the longest time it was just Mom and me. But now that Mom was married, it was just me. I was ashamed of myself most of the time. I really didn't know how to shake off the shame. Was it even possible to shake off my reputation and start fresh, like Andy? Was it possible to be respected? It felt weird just thinking about that.

This book was forcing me to think of a lot of things. I finished reading it, late the next day.

When I went to put the book back on the shelf as per the maid's instructions, another book fell out.

'Anne Frank The Diary of a Young Girl.'

I was unsure whether I should read it or not. I was a boy. I was someone who bullied others. Why would I want to read the diary of a young girl? But then I realized maybe I would like to know what lay in the minds of girls. Such a mysterious species. Reading the back of the book convinced me to read it. And it would forever change my life.

Anne Frank wanted the diary to be her friend. I realized that I, who had no friends whatsoever, could do the same. I looked down at the notebook and started scribbling.

Right this moment, I feel a sense of peace and lightness. It is a little unbearable and frightening at the same time. I feel as if I was being crushed before, and then, someone removed all that weight, instantly. Every breath makes me shake, just a little. I touch my face because I cannot stop smiling.
I finally have a friend. You, Mr. Diary.
And like Anne Frank who called her diary Kitty, I will also give you a name. I will call you Tommy.
Thank you for giving me this idea, Anne.
Later,
Wayne

The maid interrupted me when it was time for lunch. She surprised me. I had lost track of time. I hadn't been able to stop reading.

I thought of Anne Frank, and for the first time, felt sadness for someone other than my mom.

I looked at the back of the book and realized that Anne Frank had been killed by Hitler's men. I knew about Hitler. We had talked about him in History. But this was the first time I was struck by the terrorizing impact he had on a child. Someone my age. I wrote in my diary again.

Tommy, so what if children die? Those children could grow up to say mean things behind my back. Or become men who hurt my mom.

Like Anne Frank, I realized I had also hidden myself within myself.

Tommy, I am realizing that I have been so afraid of being hurt that I have successfully hid behind the persona of a bully. It has kept me safe, except for that one time when Andy punched me.
But after this summer break, I am starting a new school. Maybe it is time that I let go of my outer shell.
Maybe I don't need to hide anymore. Maybe hiding is not good.
Anne Frank hid because she had to. Otherwise, she would have been killed. She would have given anything to be free and to not hide anymore.
I think I should refuse to hide anymore.
For her.
What do you think, Tommy? Should I do it?

Reading Anne Frank's words made me jittery. Hitler was a bully who was responsible for the death of millions of people. Realizing that I was also a bully made me want to jump out of my skin.

Tommy, when does bullying really begin?

When I look at my own life, I know that most people at my school call me a bully. Hopefully, soon to be my old school. I know my actions classify me as a bully. I know I am an angry boy.

The earliest I remember being angry was when I was five years old. My mom was crying. I was playing with something. I don't remember what I was playing with, but I remember what Mom was wearing.

A pale green, sleeveless dress that stopped at her knees. Her mascara had mingled with her tears and formed dark rings around her eyes. She screamed suddenly and threw a pillow at me. It didn't strike me, but it startled me. I remember looking at her, waiting for her to comfort me like she always did. But she didn't. Not this time. Instead, she screamed some more and stormed out of the room.

I remember not being able to breathe very well when she stormed out of the room. I stood up and ran behind her. When I caught up with her, she was still crying. I yanked at her dress and she turned around and screamed again.

"Go away, go away, go away. Leave me alone."

I caught the intensity but not the emotion behind her yells, and I did the only thing a five-year-old can do.

I screamed at the top of my lungs. I was angry. I was hungry. More than anything else, I wanted my mother to comfort me. I was used to getting hugs and lots of love, and instead, I felt rejected.

That first outburst set the tone for me. I realized that anger got me things. In that instance, my mother instantly calmed down and caught me up in her arms.

First day of kindergarten: I was one of the tiniest children. Some of the other kids would kick me, shove me aside, and even call me names. Sometimes the teacher thought it was "cute." Other times she thought it was "funny."

One day, I screamed at the top of my voice when one of the "cute" little girls had punched me in the stomach again.

That got the teacher's attention and the little girl went from "cute" to "bad girl."

I soon realized I could go one step higher by initiating the hurting. When I was the one doing all the hurting, the other kids stopped bothering me.

When one of the teachers scolded me for bullying, I learned to do it when none of the adults were around. Pretty soon, I didn't know how to be anything different. The kids were always uneasy around me and I liked that power.

But being like Hitler, who was a mass murderer and was responsible for Anne Frank's death, does not make me feel nice, Tommy.

I am seriously rethinking this bully thing. So what if someone decides to hurt me? Or worse, take a punch at me? Andy already did, and I survived.

And I survived MRSA. I am a warrior. I don't need to hide. Or be scared. I don't think Anne Frank would approve of bullies.

Professor Morrie said, "We don't see what we could be." Maybe I don't see who or what I am going to end up becoming, but I know that I don't want to be a bully anymore.

Later,

Wayne

When Mom came in to ask me if I was joining her and Eugene for dinner, I realized the sun would be setting soon. I was not done reading the book yet.

It took me another couple of days before I finished reading about Anne Frank. There were a few times I had to put the book down because it made me really sad. Once I had finished reading it, I had to read it all over again, start to finish. I had never done that with a book before.

CHAPTER 4
DARTS

A few things happened that summer that would quite literally change my life completely. A new school, and darts, not in that order.

I was exploring our new house. Mom was out shopping, again. Eugene had gone to the yacht club. Our housekeeper, Martha, was in the kitchen. I was opening and closing doors until I opened the door to a room labeled the DEN. It had a pool table, a TV that took up almost an entire wall, and a dartboard.

Right as I walked up to the dartboard, I heard a noise.

It was Martha, and she had two glasses on a tray. "Have lemonade, yeah?" she asked.

After I took a glass, she took the other one and then said, "I was Dart throwing champion in my country."

I looked at Martha and couldn't imagine her as a champion in anything. She was our housekeeper.

She scrunched up her nose at me and said with a laugh, "Well, I not always fat, Wayne. Now you look my body and you think, Martha, where are you, get outa' there."

She laughed again. I did too.

Martha continued, "I was fit, long years ago. Play darts all day long, every day. Nobody beat me."

She then picked up a few darts and then threw them one, two, three. All three met bull's eye.

"Wow," I said, "can you show me how to do that?"

"Of course, I show you. But you do what I tell you to do, yeah?"

Now, this was going to be difficult. I really didn't like doing what I was told to do. It wasn't personal. It was just who I was.

However, Martha took the decision out of my hands. She did not give me an option. Taking me by the hand and walking out of the den, she said, "I give you exercise you do every day. It's easy peasy simple. Come to backyard."

Martha led me out of the house and into the backyard. She made me sit in one of the deck chairs. "Wait," she said, and walked away from me and towards a tree. She stuck a colorful dart in the tree and started walking back towards me. "Focus on dart for five minutes." She fiddled with her phone. "My timer make noise, you get up from chair and we go inside."

I looked at the dart in the distance and knew that it would be easy for me to keep my focus on that little dart. I had imagined being a body in outer space so many times that I knew exactly what I had to do. I imagined that I was the dart. I felt the breeze moving through my feathers. I looked at the sunlight covering the dart on all sides and felt that it was me that the sun was actually warming. I looked at the tree and imagined my face pressed into it. I could almost smell the bark of the tree.

Martha's timer went off at that time.

"Very nice, Wayne," said Martha, laughing loudly. "I expecting you are not so good. Children young like you cannot focus good. You start very, very young to learn focus like that. I am impressed. You are good. Come, I show you now to throw the darts."

I followed Martha into the house and back to the den.

Half an hour later, Martha had proclaimed me a natural. Although I hadn't made bull's eye yet, she said I had shown a lot of promise. I had never missed the board.

"Martha, I really want to be a dart throwing champion." I swallowed past a lump the size of a boulder stuck in my throat and said, "I will do everything you tell me to do. Do you think you could help me become a champ?"

Martha clapped her hands and smiled until she had tears in her eyes.

That made me uncomfortable. I swallowed hard and was about to ask her why she was crying, when she volunteered that information, "I always want. Want to be national champion. To be world champion. But I leave my country and come to America for better life. Then, no darts. I work, work, work. All the time." She blew her nose loudly into a tissue, and continued, "I have chance with you. I help you become champion. Follow me, Wayne." She walked out of the den. I had to run to keep up with her long stride.

Martha took out a notepad and pen from her apron pocket and started scribbling something and then handed it to me.

Martha's cooking recipe to be national dart throwing champion
Learn Focus.
Meditate. Help you not think other things when you throw darts in competition.
Make strong wrists.
Make strong legs.
Eat good.
Drink water. Lots.
Run 5 miles every day.
Make pull-ups every day.
Make push-ups every day.
Lift weights.
Rope skip.
Practice throw darts every day.

That night, right before going to bed, I took out my diary and started writing.

Dear Tommy,

I feel like I am molting. I am discarding the old feelings of not good enough, of shame, anger, and disgust.

I have yet to get used to my "new skin" of happiness, and of wanting to accomplish something. I am becoming good friends with Martha, even though she is very old. She is 50. Life feels very nice, Tommy. I never knew it could be like this.

Until next time,
Wayne

While Mom and Eugene settled into married life and doing the round of parties and socializing with other married couples, Martha and I stuck to our training regimen.

Martha said, "Everything you doing make you champion or not. Yeah? This you doing every day. New habits, okay?"

"Yes, Martha," I said with a smile.

"You know how many days to make new habits?" Martha asked me.

"21 days," I said quickly. I remember Mom reading something to me from one of her women's magazines about this.

"Well," Martha started saying, although her accent made it sound like "veil, you need little more time than that. Maybe 66 days for some habits. So, yeah. Be kind to you. Not good idea to make this new habit for just one day or two days. Make new habits for rest of life. Keep in mind always, okay?"

I nodded and smiled at Martha. I practiced the Focus exercise every single day.

I started meditating. That was difficult for me, as Martha wanted me to empty my head of all thoughts, even the ones where I pretended to be a dart or the breeze or the cushion that I was sitting on, while meditating.

While she cooked me different meals every day, I would take two cans of coconut milk, and holding them in each hand, flex my wrists. I would do this for several repetitions at a time. I went into the exercise room and started exercising my calf muscles and my feet, all under Martha's supervision. I did pull-ups and push-ups. Martha made sure I ate well and drank a few liters of water every day.

Learning to run was hard. I was overweight and hated exercise. Initially, Martha and I just walked around the block. We walked our way up to five miles. She had me run for a minute and then walk for five minutes. Soon, I was running more and more minutes until I was running all five miles. It took me a month, but I was running five miles, doing five pull-ups and 10 push-ups, without dying. As soon as I was able to do the five-mile run, Martha had me skip rope. Starting at one minute, we worked our way up to ten minutes.

And of course, my favorite part of the whole exercise routine was the actual dart throwing. I started out by throwing darts really close to the dartboard. When I made bull's eye every single time without missing even one attempt, Martha had me move six inches away from the dartboard. By the time summer was over, I could throw darts and make bull's eye from as far away as 15 feet. Since regulations dictate throwing darts from seven or eight feet away, I practiced from that distance too, every single day.

Everything I was doing to fashion myself into a dart throwing champion, Martha was also doing. She was coach and player at the same time.

The evening finally arrived when we had set up an exhibition match for Mom and Eugene. The greatest day of my life. Not only did I make bull's eye every single time, I made bull's eye blindfolded too. I had been practicing that when Martha was busy in the kitchen and I had some time to myself. I would look at the dartboard, face it, blindfold myself, and pretend to be the dart that I would throw. When the dart hit the board, I cringed because I could feel it on my face.

Mom and Eugene made one last trip to Paris before school started that Fall. Martha didn't like to drive, so if we had to drive somewhere, we would Uber our way there and back.

It was one such drive, and the driver had left a box of darts on the back seat.

As soon as I got in, I picked up the box and said, "Your darts are on the back seat." When I saw the brand name, I asked, "Do you like this brand?"

"You play darts? I didn't know kids played darts anymore. Yeah, that's my favorite brand," the driver replied.

"Do you compete?" I asked excitedly.

"Nah. I'm not that good. But I got myself a blowgun and that can make my darts go faster and farther."

"Martha, have you ever used a blowgun?"

Martha shook her head.

The driver spoke up again and said, "I carry my blowgun and darts everywhere, little man. Urban survival, Moana style."

I laughed. I had seen that movie. The villainous little people had used a blow dart and felled the big warrior – played by 'the Rock'.

"I want one of those blowguns. Where did you get yours?" I asked the driver.

"Here, I have an extra one. It's used, but at least you will have one right away. Just $20."

I finally had money. Well, Mom did, and she was always giving me $20 bills. I took a $20 bill out of my pocket and handed it to the driver.

When we got back home that evening, it took some time before I successfully managed to use the blowgun. I blew darts at the dart board from clear across the room. Martha had set up target practice in the back yard as well. I was trying to see how far I could go and still use the blowgun. I got up to 30 feet before the dart fell short of the target.

Besides throwing darts, I learned something about self-defense that would come in handy, very soon.

Parents give many reasons for forcing their children to learn martial arts – a big one being, self-defense is good to build self-confidence.

Eugene had served for decades in the Marines and there were parts of his active duty he still didn't divulge to anyone. Mom had tried hard to get him to open up, but he hadn't.

All Mom had told him about changing schools was that Andy had punched me and the Principal at the other school had done nothing to punish Andy.

In a rush of mistaken and misplaced paternalistic feelings, Eugene felt compelled to impart some of his martial arts training to me.

He showed me where to press on a man's neck to knock the breath out of him and possibly get him to pass out. He had me practice on him several times, even after I got it right.

I snuck up behind Mom one evening, and when I pressed down on her neck, I could literally feel her take a breath and then stop breathing altogether. I quickly let go before she passed out. When she turned around, I was so afraid she would reprimand me, I said quickly, "Eugene wanted me to know ways of protecting myself. And I wanted you to know that I have this knowledge."

CHAPTER 5
GUNS

In addition to teaching me how to sneak up behind someone and render them unconscious, Eugene also took me to the shooting range for some target practice.

I knew my aim was good. The dartboard had shown me that. I had expected I would have the same luck with guns. But it was a different beast altogether.

"Eugene," I asked my step-dad, "I know I have the target in my sights. If this were a dart, I would have hit that target. What am I doing wrong?"

Eugene smiled at me and said, "Great observation, Wayne. You are missing your target because you are flinching right before you fire the gun. You are anticipating the recoil, son, and when you flinch before you fire, it affects your target."

"How can I stop flinching?" I asked, wondering if that was even possible.

Eugene said, "Practice a lot."

Even though I was excited to shoot guns at the range, there was something about shooting that made me uncomfortable. I felt that a 14-year-old boy should not be handling weapons. I couldn't help but think of all the shootings that took place every single day. School shootings, gang violence, gun incidents in private homes, both accidental and deliberate, mass shootings in churches, malls, and even outdoor concerts.

In spite of my mixed feelings on shooting, I was still excited to hold a gun AND get to fire it. Target practice at the shooting range taught me something about myself that I wasn't aware of. I was super-competitive. Who knew? So even though I had never shot guns before, I could not bear to not hit the target.

Over the next few weeks, I got a crash course in guns. Eugene never let me handle any of the guns unless he was present. And I never knew where he kept the guns or the bullets. Although Eugene had a collection of guns going as far back as some kind of a rifle from the Civil War, he was also of the firm belief that guns were not for everyone.

"Why not?" I asked him, not knowing that it would lead to more than an hour of back and forth, but without any clear answers.

"What can you remember about gun ownership that didn't turn out so good?"

"Phillips Bay," I said, the name of the recent high school with a shooting tragedy.

Even though I didn't know any of the kids at that school, I couldn't help shuddering when I contemplated that it could very well have been me. "That could have been a gunman at my school," I said.

Eugene put his arm around my shoulders and said, "I am glad it wasn't, kid. But Phillips Bay is one very important and urgent reason to not have guns in everyone's hands."

"What if the teachers had been armed? They could have stopped the massacre from getting worse, couldn't they?" I asked Eugene.

"What?!!" Eugene exploded in anger. "Who the hell is teaching you these things?"

I hadn't known Eugene that long. Just a few months, really. But in all that time, I had never heard him raise his voice or be angry. Not once.

I tried not to be cowed by his anger. Besides, I was really curious.

"I'm just a kid and I want to know," I said.

That calmed him down a little.

"Wayne, remember what I said earlier?" Eugene looked at me. I looked back. After a minute of silence, I realized he was expecting an answer. My mind raced, trying to figure out what it was that Eugene wanted me to recall.

When I finally remembered, I said quickly, "Guns are not for everyone."

"Exactly. Do you think the kid who walked in and shot kids at Phillips Bay was sane?"

That was an easy question and I almost didn't answer it until I realized that Eugene wanted his answer. So, I looked at him and said, "No."

For weeks after the shooting incident at Phillips Bay, the news had been about the school shooter's mental illness.

"People are people, Wayne. Just like there are crazy kids or crazy adults who shouldn't have guns, there could be crazy teachers who shouldn't have guns. Now, who do we know whose job it is to carry guns?"

I knew the answer. "Cops," I said cheerfully, happy to know the answer.

"You are exactly right. Tell me, do cops end up killing innocent people?"

I knew this answer too. "Oh yes, definitely," I said, not so cheerfully this time.

"Now, cops go through extensive training to learn how to fire and when to fire before they officially become cops. Their job is to protect us. Their job is to protect ALL of us regardless of race, age, wealth, and status. Why do you think they make mistakes and end up killing innocent people?"

I thought about this too before answering Eugene. Every time Eugene said something, it sounded so thoughtful, as if he had considered what he was going to say and measured out how many words he wanted to use. He inspired me to think a bit before I said anything too.

I finally looked at Eugene and said, "They are afraid."

"Exactly," said Eugene.

"And when you are afraid," I continued, "you don't always make the right decision." I knew this because of my bullying background. I was afraid of being hurt and that fear had turned me into a bully. I didn't like where it took me. Into a hospital with a life-threatening MRSA infection, and out of a school I had grown comfortable with. I had no friends and no support system at my old school. Yeah, fear didn't work out very well for me.

Eugene was very happy with my answer. He smiled and said, "Very insightful answer, son. Now, tell me what happened at Phillips Bay! Did they have an armed security guard?"

"Yes, they did. But he didn't do anything for the first five minutes."

"Why is that, Wayne? He had a gun and he was a trained cop."

"He was too afraid." But then I thought of all the training he must have received before becoming a cop and I asked

Eugene, "Does that mean he didn't get good training to be a cop?"

Eugene laughed at first and then, frowning a little, he said, "No, Wayne. It means he's human."

I was surprised Eugene had said that, being an ex-Marine and all. I didn't realize I had said that out loud until Eugene said, "No matter how much training you have received, you are not going to know how you will react or respond, whether you will pull the trigger or cower behind someone, until you are pushed into action. We are all humans. We can make mistakes."

That totally didn't make sense to me. So, I said as much to Eugene and asked him, "Why do police academies exist then? Why do people go through training?"

"Wayne, think about it. We make these mistakes **after** we go through all this training. Imagine how terrible we would be if we didn't go through the training to be cops or marines or seals or whatever else!"

He had a point there. I scratched my head, trying to remember why we were talking about all this, and then I remembered my original question of whether there should be armed teachers at a school.

Eugene wasn't done. He asked, "What do you think happens when there is an active shooter in the building or on school grounds?"

"We go on lockdown," I said.

"What do you think the shooter is thinking?"

I was totally unprepared for that question. I said, "I thought you would ask me what the armed teacher or the armed cop would be thinking."

"We can talk about that too. But first, tell me what YOU think is going through the shooter's mind."

I am ashamed to say this one felt like an easy one for me. Like I said before, I knew I was a bully. I blurted out, "He must feel like a bully."

"Very good. Keep going," Eugene encouraged me.

"He must feel a lot of power knowing he has a weapon that could kill people he hates. Really hates. People that made him feel less. People who must have made him feel horrible inside."

I was saying all this not because I knew what was inside a school shooter's mind, but because I knew why I bullied and what I was afraid of, if I didn't bully.

"Must have made him feel, Wayne? Can someone really make you feel something?"

"Of course," I said. "When people treat you horribly, it can make you feel really bad. Like you are dog poop or something disgusting."

"No, no, no, Wayne. No one can MAKE YOU feel anything. Ah, maybe you are too young to really get this, but only you can make yourself feel a certain way. No one else can make you do anything. You make yourself do or feel. Make sense?"

I shook my head. I totally did not get that. "Are you saying that the Phillips Bay school shooter made himself feel bad? I thought the kids at his school were not nice to him."

"Are you blaming the kids?" Eugene asked me. He sounded really surprised.

I thought about it before answering. "No, I am not blaming the school kids. I know they are the real victims. But what if the school kids had been nice to that shooter?"

"It's not the kids' behavior that made him a shooter, Wayne," said Eugene. "He was mentally ill. Mentally ill people should not have access to guns. That's simple logic."

"The news kept repeating he was a psychopath," I said.

"You're right. That was the mental health diagnosis," said Eugene.

I interrupted Eugene and said, "Okay, let me get this straight. No sane person, child or grown up would start shooting at school children. Right?"

"Yes and no," said Eugene emphatically. "What about hate crimes based on racism or extreme religious fundamentalism? Are those people mentally ill?"

"They're not?" I asked incredulously. This discussion was getting really confusing.

"I would call them brainwashed," said Eugene. "No matter how they get brainwashed, they feel justified in their feelings of hatred. Do you know why people feel that way?"

This was an easy one for me. "Yes," I said, "it's because they feel ignored and insulted."

"A little more complicated than that, son," said Eugene, patting me on the head. "They feel excluded or there haven't been reparations for past crimes or insults against them. Or their present circumstances are humiliating, denigrating, and demoralizing."

"And they have access to guns," I said.

"Exactly," said Eugene. "Earlier, you seemed to think that having armed teachers in schools would protect the school."

"Yes," I said hesitatingly, not wanting Eugene to get angry again.

"Tell me," Eugene said slowly, "how will teachers know the right way to shoot guns?"

I laughed, because the question was so simple.

"They will receive training," I said.

There was a brief silence before Eugene said abruptly, "We just talked about cops making mistakes and shooting innocent people, even after receiving extensive training. Can armed teachers make those mistakes too?"

I thought about it before saying, "Yes, I think so. Actually, they might make way more mistakes."

"Exactly," said Eugene. "And remember what I said earlier about crazy teachers?"

When there was silence, I realized Eugene was waiting for me to respond.

"Yes, I remember. You said some of the teachers could be crazy and they shouldn't have guns," I said.

Before Eugene could ask me anything else, I asked him a question that was bothering me. "Is it ok to say crazy? Do you mean to say mentally ill?"

Eugene looked at me, actually looked at me, before shaking his head and giving me an embarrassed laugh. "Out of the mouth of babes. You're right, son, I should've said mentally ill and not crazy. I just revealed my own bias."

I asked another question, "If they are mentally ill and they do bad things, is it because they forgot to take their pills, their medicine?"

Eugene shook his head sadly and said, "That is a possibility, son. That' is a possibility. Or, maybe the pills stopped working. Maybe the diagnosis was the wrong one. Or maybe they just stop taking the pills."

There was silence for a moment, before Eugene looked at me and said, "Let's table this mental illness bit for a second. Tell me, what if there is an active shooting, and cops storm into the school and see a teacher with a gun? Could they shoot the teacher?"

"Yes," I said. "That would not be good at all."

"Yes, it most certainly would not be good," said Eugene. "It gets worse, son. What if a kid brings a toy gun to school and pretends to shoot? It would be the height of stupidity for anyone to do that, I know. But let's say a kid does that. What if, in a rush of adrenaline, the teacher shoots that kid?"

I put my head in my hands and said, "This is so complicated. I thought having armed teachers in school would mean safety for us."

"Well, now you know better," said Eugene. "Go ahead and make two lists for me: one with your prior reasons to have armed teachers in schools, and the other with the reasons not to have armed teachers. Take five to do it, son."

Eugene handed me a blank sheet of paper and his pen. I started writing.

<u>Reasons to have armed teachers at school</u>
1. They can protect us from shooters.
2. They can deter others from trying to become shooters at our school.
3. They can make us feel safe on a daily basis.

<u>Reasons to NOT have armed teachers at school</u>
1. Teachers have not gone to cop school. How much training is enough to make them comfortable with having two roles at school: that of a teacher and that of a cop?
2. Cops respond to active shooters: what if they come into the school and see a teacher with a gun? Will they shoot that teacher?
3. What if the teacher shoots an innocent student? You know, a kid who is just goofing off with a fake gun and the teacher shoots him?
4. What if a cop surprises a teacher when there is an active shooter situation in school, and the teacher shoots the cop?
5. What if the teacher is mentally ill and has not been diagnosed or has not taken the right medicine for

his/her mental illness or has stopped taking medicine?

It took me a lot longer than five minutes to write all that down, and longer even to turn in the page to Eugene. As I handed it over to him, I asked, "Eugene, what do you think the armed cops are thinking when they are trying to find the school shooter?"

Eugene shook his head sadly and said, "They're probably petrified of shooting innocent children or of the shooter killing more people or even of getting shot at."

"What is the real solution if it's not more guns inside the school?" I asked.

Eugene glanced over at my sheet of paper, before sitting on the couch and saying, "Responsible gun ownership. Lock up guns in a safe, secure place so kids don't have access to them."

I knew kids were not the only ones shooting innocent people. So, I said a little defensively, "But that doesn't solve the problem of adults shooting people in malls or outdoor concerts."

Eugene looked up from my sheet of paper and said, "You are absolutely right, son. A few of our states have *red flag laws* that allow law enforcement to confiscate the guns of those people who are thought to be at risk of harming themselves or others."

That was news to me. But something bothered me a little and I asked Eugene, "How does law enforcement find out if these people are a risk?"

Eugene smiled and said, "That's a terrific question, son. Some cases will be obvious based on social media rantings or because a family member or community member catches on and calls the police. But I imagine there will be other cases, son, where we may not know until it's too late."

"But there has to be more we can do, right? More than the red flag laws?" I asked.

Eugene patted me on the head and said, "Yup, there's more. Instead of creating an environment that excludes a certain section of society, we have to set up a system of collaboration and a genuine desire to help one another. We need more mental health screenings, interventions, follow ups and vigilance. Everyone, including teachers, should have access to great mental health care. Instead of training some teachers to be armed shooters, how about we train them to recognize signs of mental illness?"

Eugene paused for a bit before continuing, "Son, we know so little about mental health and the resources that already exist. Do you know there are national hotline numbers we can call for information regarding mental health issues? I actually feel we need more than that."

"More than a number that you call for information?" I asked Eugene.

"Yes, son," said Eugene. "In this day and age of telemedicine, we should be able to set up several national, hotline numbers and have it staffed 24/7 with well-paid, well-trained, mental health professionals who can actually take you through therapy or send someone to your house, depending on how serious the situation is. I really don't know the logistics and legalities involved, but I feel it's time that we do something different from what we have been doing already."

Mom walked in right as he was saying all that. She kissed Eugene and then walked towards me and kissed me, before saying, "I love what you are saying, but how do we get past the stigma of mental illness? It's all well and good that we have these hotline numbers. But, how do we get people to actually pick up the phone and call? And let's not forget payment. Who is paying for these calls? Are they free or does insurance cover the cost?"

Eugene smiled lovingly at Mom and said, "Those are the answers everyone wants to have."

Mom ruffled my hair and asked, "Excited to go to school tomorrow?"

Meh. It was a new school, which made me happy because I wouldn't have to see Andy or hear any of the other kids ask me if I was happy Andy had saved my life! Mom looked so hopeful when she asked me that question, I did not have the heart to tell her I was indifferent. So, I said, "Yes, Mom, I am."

She clapped her hands happily. It was nice to finally see Mom looking like someone was taking great care of her. She no longer looked as worried as she used to.

Tommy,

Eugene and I had a great conversation today. But I still don't know how we can stop mentally ill people from buying guns. I still don't know how to stop people from feeling hatred.

I know now that my dad's brutality had filled me with anger and hatred. How do I change the past so I remove all that hatred from my insides? And how many people in my school or city or country or the world are walking around with hate in their hearts? Are they all waiting for someone to pull their trigger?

Tommy, how do we remove the hate that people feel?

Eugene is nice to Mom and me. Life is great.

Martha said I have to start thinking about 'paying it forward,' which means doing something good for others. I don't know how to do this.

I overheard Mom say that Eugene has many "wonderful qualities" and I agree. He is extremely rich. He is healthy. He has great friends. He is a happy man, and he is incredibly generous to us.

I remember someone once saying that you can judge a man by what his employees think of him. Martha adores and respects him tremendously.

I have two words for you, Tommy. Role model.

To be continued,

Wayne

CHAPTER 6
NOBEL PRIZE WINNERS

It was my first day at my new school. My chance at creating a new persona. A new reputation. But that was not what I was thinking as I climbed the steps to the school. What I was thinking was that I had never had reason to be afraid of bullies. I had always been the bully at my old school.

But now that Anne Frank had convinced me not to hide, I had resolved to just be me, which was really who I was around Mom. I loved doing things for her. I loved being kind to her. I loved to make her smile and laugh. I did not want to bully anymore, but I also did not want to be bullied. So, I still tried to come across as a tough guy.

When I walked into the school, I made eye contact with as many kids as I could. I nodded at them but did not smile. I didn't want people to think I was friendly or weak. I was anxious to see how the new school kids would treat me.

I was an eighth grader. I knew that at 14 years old, I would be one of the oldest in my class. I liked that because I knew that would also make me one of the taller and bigger kids.

As soon as I walked into my classroom, I walked to the back, ready to claim the seat farthest away from the teacher. I had just sat down when this absolutely pale girl walked in. She was goth, wearing all black, with dramatic, black make-up, and multiple piercings on each ear, and one on her right nostril. She walked right up to me and gave me a smile.

If you looked past all her piercings and the eye make-up, her eyes were a clear blue and her smile was so wide, it lit up the space around her. If my heart hadn't started beating erratically, I would have said something. Anything.

She filled the awkward silence with her laughter and said, "I'm Maisy. My parents know Eugene and they said to help you if necessary, since it's your first day here."

I did not utter a word. I couldn't. I was too embarrassed to even clear my throat, as I felt that would make my self-consciousness very obvious.

She waited a few seconds. When I didn't say anything, she said, "Anyway, nice to meet you, Wayne. I will see you around."

As soon as she exited, my tongue unstuck itself from the roof of my mouth. I said softly, "See you around."

Just then our teacher walked in and put her bag down at the front of the classroom. Instead of sitting on her chair at the front, she walked up and down the aisles. When she got to me, she smiled at me, and said, "Hello, you must be Wayne Benko. New kid on the block. I'm Mrs. Tripp. Welcome to my Math class."

She walked back up to the front of the classroom and asked, "Who can tell me the name of the Nobel Prize winner in Math for 2018?"

Out of the corner of my eye, I saw an arm fluttering desperately, obviously trying to catch Mrs. Tripp's attention.

She smiled and said, "Yes, Krish, tell me."

"There is no Nobel Prize in Math. There is the Fields medal instead and an Australian of Indian descent, Akshay Venkatesh won it in 2018."

She clapped her hands, her smile getting wider.

"Okay, my math geniuses, do you think Akshay Venkatesh ever fell asleep in his middle school Math class?"

The class erupted in laughter and shouts of "Yes," "No," and "Maybe."

I laughed too, and immediately sat up straighter. I wanted to pay attention. The class period went by fast. When the school bell rang, Mrs. Tripp said, "Remember, there is no progress without children doing really well in school, and that means all of you bright young things need to be the future stars. So, pay attention and enjoy learning. See you tomorrow."

While waiting for the next teacher, my mind wandered to thoughts of what I would have done at my old school.

I used to like the rush of feeling I got when I intimidated someone. Sure, I knew I was bullying them. I knew that if I didn't bully them, they would bully me. It was far better to be the aggressor than to be aggressed.

I wondered what Mrs. Tripp thought of bullies or of ex-bullies. Even as I was thinking that, I couldn't help but revert to habit. If I had stopped to think about it, I would have remembered that I had resolved not to bully. I would have remembered the impact Anne Frank had made on me.

Instead, I remembered that I had darts in my bookbag. And a blowgun. I took the blowgun out along with one of the darts, and looked around. I looked at Krish. I had a trick. I pretended that his elbow was the bull's eye and I pretended to blow the dart towards the bull's eye. I saw the trajectory of the dart a few times before I finally let the dart free. Off it went and BULL'S EYE. Well, it would have been bull's eye, if Krish hadn't moved his hand at the last second. The dart embedded itself into one of his books and Krish yanked it out.

"Wow, what a beautiful dart," exclaimed Krish.

I was surprised to hear praise from someone who had just been attacked.

And I was not the only one surprised. One of the other kids in the classroom laughed and said, "Trust you to be curious even about something that tries to harm you."

Krish was holding up the dart and saying, "Look at its shape. This aerodynamic feature along with the tiny feathers and the length of the tail gives it its ability to be used as a projectile. If used with a blowgun at close quarters and with sufficient force, it could really hurt someone."

As I was about to send another dart at someone else, I remembered my promise to not be a bully anymore. Oh boy! Day one and I had already failed.

The girl immediately to Krish's right said, "Whoever brought this in could get expelled. Krish, are you going to report this?"

Krish just laughed and said, "No. Someone's just having fun. No one was harmed."

Although I was glad Krish was not going to report the dart, I was thinking that he was very naïve. But what surprised me the most was how disappointed I felt in myself. What good was a goal if I couldn't even try to make it?

Maybe I was having unrealistic expectations of myself. Maybe instead of giving myself just the morning to turn over a new leaf and be a good kid, I should give myself 66 days or the rest of my life, like Martha had suggested over the summer. I took out my phone and quickly typed in a diary entry in my Notes.

Tommy,
First day of school and I have already failed.
I have to remember to write down my goals when I get home this afternoon. I had told myself I would no longer be a bully, but I

think I have to actually write it down and remind myself of it every single day. I have realized I have to also write down how I am going to meet that particular goal – i.e. write my strategy for that goal. In this case, if I don't want to be a bully any more, my strategy would be to not hurt or humiliate anyone – by words, behavior, or objects.

I am reinventing myself, Tommy. I am developing a new character and I don't think it can happen overnight.

Martha told me it takes some time to develop habits.

What is the opposite of bullying? Supporting? Whatever the opposite of bullying is, it will be a new habit for me and it won't happen overnight. It is going to take some time.

I have to remind myself of it every single day. And I will, because it is important to me that I no longer bully anyone.

Things have been so good for Mom and me. Martha said I have to pay it forward by being good to others. I don't think it will be easy for me to do that...I may have to actually remind myself every day to pay it forward.

You're cool, Tommy. Thank you for not judging. Thank you for not interrupting me, ever.

Your friend,

Wayne

As our next teacher walked into the classroom, all the kids immediately took their seats. "Good morning, Good morning. Let's see. I know about the new kid already." He looked at me and said, "Welcome. Welcome. I'm Mr. Laboy."

He then walked up to Krish and said, "I know YOU know the answer to this, Krish." Putting his hand on Krish's shoulder, he addressed the rest of us, "Let's see which one of your classmates knows the names of the Nobel Prize winners in Physiology or Medicine for 2018. And," raising his voice over the chatter that had begun, Mr. Laboy asked, "why did they win it?"

Krish was squirming in his seat. I am sure he wanted to blurt out his answer.

Finally, a girl from the front of the classroom raised her hand.

"Yes, Nathalia?" asked Mr. Laboy.

"Actually, two people won it. James Allison and Tasuku Honjo for discovering a new form of cancer therapy that involves our immune system."

"Brava, Nathalia. Now all you budding, brilliant biologists, listen up. Guess who, besides Krish here, paid attention in their Biology class?"

Everyone laughed. I heard shouts of "those two," "me," "Satoshi Nakamoto," "Nathalia," and "no one."

Mr. Laboy's class was actually pretty interesting. He talked about Molecular Biology and even though occasionally my hands twitched from wanting to throw or shoot more darts from the back of the room, the introduction to molecular biology was fascinating.

When the school bell rang and the kids started to put their books away, Mr. Laboy called out my name.

"Wayne Benko, can you come up here for a second?"

I was surprised, of course. But I walked up to him and waited for him to gather his things.

"I know your step-dad, Eugene. He asked me to make sure that you have a great, first day at school. Is everything good so far?"

"Yes, sir," I answered.

"Let me know if you need anything. Eugene thinks the world of you, you know," said Mr. Laboy, as he gathered up his things and turned to walk away, leaving me staring at him.

I really didn't know what to say to Mr. Laboy. It felt nice to have Eugene say good things about me. But, would he still feel the same way if he really knew me? Martha had always said that it is never a bad idea for a young kid to smile and say Thank you. So that's exactly what I did.

Although Mr. Laboy couldn't see me smile, I know he heard me when I called out, "Thank you, Mr. Laboy."

CHAPTER 7
SOCIAL STUDIES

By the time I walked back to my seat and sat down, the teacher walked in the door. She looked very young and very nervous.

"Please take your seats." She had to repeat herself a few times before everyone returned to their seats.

"Good morning, everyone. I'm Miss Samuels, your substitute teacher for the day."

The class was Social studies and our teacher was mind-numbingly boring.

Fifteen minutes in, I couldn't take it anymore. I walked up to the teacher and asked politely, "Miss Samuels, may I go to the Boy's room, please?"

Miss Samuels looked at me over her glasses and then, turning to the kid sitting directly in front of her own chair, she asked him, "What is your name?"

"Brock," said the kid.

"Go with Wayne and be back in five minutes. Not a minute more than that."

Boy, that was easy, I thought.

On the way to the Boy's room, I said to Brock, "You don't have to go all the way to the Boy's room with me. If you want to wait outside the classroom, I will be back here in five minutes. We just won't tell Miss Samuels."

Brock went back to stand outside the classroom. He was already lost in the Minecraft world on his phone.

I walked quickly to the lockers that were right next to the restrooms. My goal was to find out if Maisy had any secrets. My strategy for that goal was to see if I could open the lockers, find out which one was hers and get the dirt on her, and maybe even on some of the other kids in school.

Yup, that whole cultivating new habits thing. I was really relaxed about it all. I had 66 days or a lifetime, after all.

As soon as I got to the lockers, I heard the cocking of a handgun. It was a very distinctive sound. Eugene had several handguns and we had gone to the shooting range multiple times over the summer.

"Must be the school cop," was my first thought. "Why on earth is he cocking it inside the school?" was my second thought.

And then I heard someone speak. It was a boy who was obviously going through puberty. His voice was breaking, but he said very clearly, "Do you want both semi-automatics?"

"Shhh," I heard another voice, a deeper voice and also obviously male. "Keep your voice down."

And then I got it. There was going to be a shooting in my new school, and judging by what I had just heard, it would be deadly.

"Oh God, I am going to die." That was my first thought, followed by, "I wish I was still at my old school and not here, waiting to die."

And then I heard it. My chance to rush back to my classroom or at least head outside the school. I heard some voices reciting a kind of oath. Still terrified to make too much noise, I sneaked my way past the lockers and turned the corner, hoping to make it to safety soon.

As soon as I turned the corner, I saw Maisy leaving her classroom, which was all the way down the hall, immediately before my classroom. She smiled and waved at me.

I said impulsively, "Don't go anywhere. I heard some boys by the lockers. They have guns."

Maisy blanched, and her skin got even whiter. She turned back immediately. When she saw Brock standing outside my classroom, she said something to him, and the two ran into Maisy's classroom and closed the door.

Before I could move even one step, the school alarm went off and a recording came on.

"Take shelter immediately. This is not a drill. Shooters in the area. Take shelter immediately. This is not a drill."

I ran as hard as I could back to my class. The door was locked. I tried seeing in, but there was a curtain already in place and I could not see inside. I rattled the doorknob, not daring to make any noise louder than I had to. I heard laughter and realized the boys were getting closer. I ran as fast as I could, as softly as I could, not knowing where I could possibly hide.

I saw an open door and ran in. It looked like the teacher's lounge. It was quite big. I looked around wildly and saw that besides the usual kitchen appliances and dining room tables and chairs, there was also a well-stocked pantry, the doors to which were wide open.

I took my phone out and almost dialed 911, but didn't want the shooters to hear me. I was beside myself and too terrified to make the wrong, next move. Think, Wayne, think. First things first, I closed the lounge door. Softly. I was terrified of locking it, knowing they could easily shoot the door open. If it was locked from the inside, they would know someone was hiding inside. I looked around again, and saw a cleaning closet all the way towards the back of the pantry. I ran into the pantry. I opened the half open closet doors all the way and almost cried with relief when I realized I could squeeze my body into the tight space. That would not have happened without Martha's workout routine for me. I unscrewed the one light bulb in there and hid in a corner.

And waited. I could hear shots and screams in the distance.

I looked around the closet and made myself think of what could happen in case they decided to get something out of the closet. So, I arranged all the brooms in front of my hiding place, all eight of them. I then arranged the mop bucket in front of the brooms. I didn't close the pantry door or the door to the cleaning closet completely. I wanted a view of what was going on inside the teacher's lounge.

I patted the pockets in my pants and felt around for my blowgun and the darts. Thank God, I had them on me. I took my blowgun out and fitted it with a dart. I closed my eyes and imagined blowing the dart. My mouth was so dry, I was terrified I wouldn't be able to use the blowgun properly. I had to choke back nervous laughter when I realized I could probably use sweat instead of saliva. I was sweating profusely.

"Hahahahahahaha." I heard loud laughter and the lounge door burst open. I cowered behind the brooms.

"Oh, man. That was something. Who knew Mrs. Abramson would go down like that?"

I broke out in a cold sweat when I heard the boys talk about dead Mrs. Abramson like that. It brought home the fact that they were cold-blooded killers and the realization that I really wasn't safe from discovery.

I gasped and stuck a fist in my mouth.

"Why was she not locked up, anyway?"

"I never liked her, Jamie. Thank you."

"My pleasure," replied a voice that must have been Jamie's.

I counted three voices. All boys. I waited to see if there would be more.

The pantry door slammed against the wall with the force with which it was opened and I immediately almost peed myself. I knew they couldn't see me, but I also knew that could change in an instant.

"Why are you in the pantry?" The first voice asked with a laugh. I could not believe how cavalier these boys sounded. They had just killed a teacher and possibly hurt others.

"Looking for hidden teachers?" asked voice 2.

"Hahahaha," laughed voice 3 and I could hear it come closer to my hideout. Although I could hear subtle differences in the three voices, I couldn't discern which one was Jamie, the one who killed Mrs. Abramson. They all sounded similar to me.

Voice 1 said, "Bob, stop right there. Don't venture too far into the pantry. Your OCD will want to organize this whole mess."

I was a big kid, and knew there was no way the brooms in the closet would adequately hide me if they decided to open the door to the cleaning closet. I looked at my phone and made sure it was on silent. The screen was lit up with messages, all from my mom asking me where I was and if I was safe.

I then heard footsteps right outside the cleaning closet and right as a shadow fell across the little sliver of space that was the gap in the closet door, I heard police sirens. I looked at my phone. Only three minutes had passed since the school alarm had gone off. It seemed like forever.

Of course, the police would not be able to save me if the boys turned their guns on me in the next few minutes. I closed my eyes shut and even though I had never been the religious sort, I started offering prayers and saying things like, "Please get me out alive, dear God, and I will stop bullying. I promise."

The voice immediately outside my hideout said loudly, "Yes, fuck it. Now it gets interesting. Now the real fun begins. Who's with me?"

"Need you ask? NBK, fuck it," said voice 2. "What was in that drink you gave us? I really need to pee."

Voice 1 said, "Just use the bathroom quickly. But I think we should split up. Bob, since you need to pee really badly, you stay here. They don't know how many of us are on the loose. I will go upstairs and see how many I can kill. Mel, you go downstairs and start the carnage. Since they think they've categorized us all as either glory-seekers or suicidal, and working alone or in a pair, they will not be expecting three of us. So, right when they think they have Mel and me, and start releasing everyone, you go into action mode, Bob."

CHAPTER 8
OCD

There was a pause. I imagined they were caught up in the solemnity of their actions. In the next second, I heard whispered words that sounded like a chant of some sort. They had moved away from the pantry and were closer to the door of the teacher's lounge. I still managed to hear bits and pieces of their chant. They used that word again – NBK. While my brain was desperately trying to figure out what NBK meant, I could hear words like dark matter, carnage, fiery pits and inglorious glory. And then there was silence.

Holy shit! NBK meant natural born killers. I vaguely remembered that the Columbine shooters called themselves that. Realizing what NBK meant immediately put me in a higher state of terror.

I heard the door to the bathroom in the teacher's lounge open and close.

Here was my chance. I was going to make a run for it. My heart was knocking around painfully, somewhere inside me. It felt like it was in my mouth! I tiptoed out of the closet and out the pantry door, when I heard the toilet flush. I looked at how far the lounge door was and realized there was no way I was going to make it without Bob noticing me.

I tiptoed at a furious pace, back into the pantry, and closed the door just so. I ran back into my hiding space in the cleaning closet and had just leaned the door shut, when the bathroom door opened. I could see Bob through the crack in the door.

He had fiery red hair and a freckled face with a snub nose, and a small mouth. He looked strong. He also looked like he was on drugs. There were shadows under his eyes, and he kept sniffling.

My brain was racing trying to think of a rescue scenario. I abandoned the idea of using the blowgun. My mouth was so dry, I could barely even open it, let alone use it to blow darts. But I knew I had thrown so many darts over the summer that my wrist and fingers could send the dart flying, even if I were to be blindfolded. I knew all I needed was an unimpeded line at Bob's face, maybe even his eyes. He was literally staring at the door to the pantry.

"Holy shit," I thought. The boys had laughed at him and said he had OCD – obsessive compulsive disorder. I was pretty sure the pantry door was different from the way he had left it!! I immediately got into my dart-throwing stance, positioned just as I was behind the brooms. I was so thankful that I had practiced throwing darts from 15 feet away. The pantry door was about 12 feet away from where I was hiding, trembling violently. I quickly took out a dart from my pocket. The only way I could stop my shivering was when I pretended to be the dart.

I visualized the dart leaving my hand and going into Bob's left eye. I did this five times before Bob lunged towards the door. The next few seconds were the most terrifying ones of my entire life.

Bob shoved the door open with both hands and it banged against the wall. My focus was unbreakable. As soon as I had a view of the whites of Bob's eyes, I thrust open the closet door, and threw my dart. It landed in Bob's left eye. In literally the next instant as Bob had yanked the dart out of his eye, and almost destroyed my left eardrum with his bellow, I had my fingers on his neck, pressing down. If I hadn't acted immediately and taken Bob by surprise, I am sure he could have and would have overwhelmed me with his strength. I pressed down on Bob's neck until he passed out.

When I looked down at Bob's immobile body, I started shivering again. I closed my eyes and pretended to be someone who was given the job of watching what I was going to do.

I then saw myself rummaging through the contents in the cleaning closet, looking for things to tie Bob up. Nothing. Just cleaning supplies.

I ran into the lounge, and opened at least seven drawers before I found some masking tape.

Bob was starting to come around and I had to press down on his neck again. I was kind enough to take the dart out of his eye, and not knowing what to do about the blood, I forced myself to ignore it. I closed the pantry door quickly and got down to business.

I taped Bob's mouth shut, shoved him onto his belly, took off one of my shoelaces and tied his hands behind his back. I then wrapped tape around his tied hands to better hold the bindings in place. I dragged him and shoved him into the cleaning closet. I found a rag and tied it tightly around his eyes, hoping that would somehow stem the bleeding. I realized it served as a blindfold as well. I then took a deep breath and looked around, trying to calm myself. I saw Bob's gun and grabbed it quickly. I knew how to use the Glock. But before I got going, I had to do something very important.

"I love u Mom. Eugene TY 4 lovn Mom. Took down shooter #1 Bob. He is in cleaning closet. I have his gun. Looking for 2 more. Mel downstairs. Jamie upstairs. Don't know them. Last names unkn. Pl give cops my profile. Tell them I'm not active shooter." I had typed this message to my mom and hit send.

Soon, I was out of the pantry and had turned around so I could close the door, softly. I had the Glock. I had my blowgun and my darts. I could hear shots go off upstairs.

My legs almost gave out when I heard a menacing, "Who the fuck are you?" Bob was in the pantry, and I could hear Jamie upstairs, so this must be Mel, I thought. His appearance surprised me. He was short and thin, with brown hair and brown eyes and a very ordinary and clean

73

look. I mean, his was the type of face that could easily blend into the background.

I knew I didn't have time to aim and shoot. So, I said, "I am ready to kill people. I saw this gun in the teacher's lounge and grabbed it immediately. Looks like you have the same idea. Let me join the fun."

Mel looked suspiciously at me and intently at the Glock.

"Is this yours?" I asked, as I moved closer to him. "It was on this table here. But what is that in your hands? Is that another Glock? Is that one fully automatic? What a beauty!" Right as I got within touching distance of Mel, I put one hand on his right shoulder and the other hand on his gun.

"Whoa," I started to say and in the same breath, I pressed down on Mel's neck. He went out like a light.

I pretended to be someone else again, as I tied Mel's hands behind his back with my other shoelace, wrapped tape around his tied hands, taped his mouth shut, and dragged him into the bathroom and left him there. I dumped his gun in the large trashcan by the lounge door.

Two down. One more to go. I texted my Mom again. I saw at least five more messages from her but did not have time to read any of them.

"Tied up 2 shooters. Have Bob's gun. Mel's gun in trashcan by lounge door. Have to find Jamie. Love u." Letting someone know what was happening made me feel better.

I was terrified. I am not going to tell you otherwise. But I kept moving because I was too afraid of staying put. I hated surprises. I felt I'd much rather surprise Jamie than be surprised by him. I heard a barrage of shots upstairs and some screams. That's how I knew for sure that he was still upstairs.

I took the stairs up two at a time and cautiously entered the hallway. My heart plummeted to my feet when I saw Jamie, his back to me, reloading his gun.

I took careful aim and shot once. I was aiming for his left knee. I got his calf, instead. Down he went, screeching loudly and screaming obscenities.

I was thankful for all that shooting practice Eugene and I did over the summer.

Jamie still had a hold of his gun and had it pointed straight at me, his face twisted in pain as well as rage. The next few seconds will forever be etched in my memory, from the saliva spitting out of Jamie's mouth as he bellowed in frustration, to his fumbling to reload his gun. I took my blowgun out and fitted it with a dart. I gave myself one chance, as I mentally marked my target.

Practice makes perfect. Thank God for it. I had practiced being the dart so many times, I became the dart as I let it fly. I saw the area below Jamie's right eye clearly. It's all I saw.

When I pierced into that skin, I felt the impact on my face and strangely enough, on my right arm. I looked at Jamie. He had tossed his gun away. One hand was holding onto his injured leg, and the other hand was trying to feel around for the dart. I realized he was squeamish about pulling it out. He hadn't once stopped screaming obscenities at me.

I felt a throbbing and burning sensation in my throwing arm. I looked at it and watched in horror at the growing splotch of red on that arm. I couldn't believe I had been shot. I had never imagined that would ever happen to me.

When I started to feel lightheaded, I looked over at Jamie, who was now writhing in pain on the floor. The dart was still embedded in his face. When he saw me look at him, he tried to crawl his way to his gun which was close enough for him to get to, and screeched, "You are not so invincible, are you? I am going to kill you. Slowly. I will then annihilate the others."

I was grateful for Jamie's words, because it snapped me out of my disbelief and self-indulgent pity. I ran and picked up his gun from the floor, pointed it at him, and said, "Not today."

I then called 911.

"911, what is your emergency?"

"Ma'am, this is Wayne Benko, calling from Dolphin Bay Academy. I caught all three of the shooters. We are safe. Please send the cops in. And Ma'am, I have been shot."

To say that the next few hours went by in a blur would be the understatement of my entire life.

The cops swarmed in. When they first arrived, they had their helmets on and their guns drawn.

As soon as they saw me, they yelled belligerently, exactly like in the movies, "Put down the gun RIGHT NOW. RIGHT NOW. RIGHT NOW. Put your hands up."

I immediately did what they asked me to. "Don't shoot. Please don't shoot. Please. I'm innocent. Help me. Please." I was frantically trying to convince the officers that I was innocent. I had my hands up in the air and I was screaming at the top of my voice.

"I'm one of the good guys. Please don't shoot me." I had bullied others for so long, it felt weird to call myself a good guy.

When the cops took the gun from me, I pointed at Mel and said, "He is the third shooter. There are two more in the teacher's lounge on the second floor. I tied their hands behind their backs and dumped one of the guns in the trashcan by the lounge door."

Some of the cops immediately ran downstairs.

The medics had rushed in now. They took the shooter out on a stretcher. He was screaming belligerently at me, "I will kill you for this. I will get you." And then he called me names I am not allowed to repeat.

Threats didn't bother me much. I had made so many of them myself over the years. For some reason, this particular threat got under my skin and I started shaking uncontrollably.

A couple of the medics ran towards me. They immediately started cutting my shirtsleeve to access my wound and stem the bleeding.

After some poking, prodding, and wiping, one of them said, "Looks like a flesh wound, kid. I am so glad the bullet just grazed you. You still need stitches, but you'll be completely healed in a week or two."

"Doctor," I said nervously, "I was in the hospital with a MRSA infection. I almost died from it. Will I get MRSA in my flesh wound?"

"When was this?" asked the doctor.

"May of this year," I said, remembering that school was almost at an end when I had been admitted to the hospital.

"Do you know how you got the MRSA?" asked the doctor, as she was stitching up the wound. It looked like a gaping tear in my arm and she was sewing me up like fabric.

"My mom carried it in her nose," I said hesitantly, not wanting anyone to judge my mom for not knowing she had MRSA in her nose.

"Thanks for telling us, son," the doctor said. "We'll talk to her and give her instructions. Don't worry."

"Doctor, the last time my wound had pus and red streaks going away from it. That turned out to be a bad thing. Could the same thing happen to me, again?" I really didn't want to be in the hospital again.

"It could happen again, son. But you can prevent it by being alert. By seeing your doctor immediately if there is redness or pus around the stitches I am putting in or pain in spite of taking pain medication or if you have a fever of 100°F or higher. Don't worry, I will give these and more instructions to your mom. We'll make sure you're okay."

I heard loud crying then and turned to see Maisy and a few of the other girls hugging each other and crying.

Some students were being carried out on stretchers. While some of them were groaning in pain, some looked lifeless.

I stared at one vaguely familiar boy as they took him past me. I couldn't tell if he was dead or just unconscious. And then I saw the bullet wound. It looked like it had gone straight through his heart.

The school bell rang harshly, signaling the end of the class period. It was at once normal and monstrous. The Social studies class period turned out to be not so boring after all. I looked up at the clock on the school wall. It was only 10:25 a.m. Time for our lunch break, which Mrs. Abramson will never take anymore.

I looked around while the medical people were finishing dressing my wound and bandaging my arm. The normalcy of the school walls covered in artwork by current and past graduates kept reminding me of the grotesque massacre that had just taken place. If children in a private school in the United States could no longer be safe....I couldn't complete that thought. I felt my stomach pitch and I threw up. I was shivering again.

Someone wrapped a blanket around me and holding me tight, kept whispering, "We got you. You're alright, kid. We got you."

I don't know who it was. They walked me outside the building.

CHAPTER 9
A HERO

"Wayne," I heard a shrill cry. It was my mother. She was standing next to the ABC TV van. She ran up to me and hugged me tight.

"My baby, my baby." She was screaming loudly.

Someone said firmly, "Your son has a flesh wound and we had to put some stitches in. He is okay. Please stay calm. That will be the best thing for him."

Someone else said, "Your son is a hero and a very lucky boy."

Mom calmed down a little. She was still crying, although not as loudly as before. The doctor walked towards us and asked my mom, "Are you his mother?"

Mom said, "Yes, Yes, I am."

The doctor said, "Nice to meet you. I am Dr. Nair. Your son has stitches which will dissolve in a week or so. He has waterproof dressing on, so he can still shower. His dressing needs to be changed sometime tomorrow. Anyone who touches his dressing, needs to first wash their hands very well and then use gloves. This goes for you, your husband, and anyone else, including your son. That's the best way we can prevent him from getting another MRSA infection." When Mom's face lost all color, the doctor quickly added, "Don't worry, he is going to be just fine."

Mom nodded. She was trying hard not to cry.

After patting my shoulder, the doctor hurried away to help some of the others.

Mom had calmed down considerably. As we were walking to her car, we passed a television van. Mom's favorite news anchor was there. Mom smiled at her, which was enough encouragement for the TV lady to approach us.

Mom, who had perked up when she saw the anchor, said eagerly, "Kris, meet my son, Wayne. He is the one who subdued the three shooters."

Kris looked at me. She had tears in her eyes and said, "You are a hero, Wayne. Can you tell us what happened in there?"

Mrs. Tripp was walking past me, and when she heard the question, she said, "You people are all vultures. Can't you leave a kid alone?" Turning to me, she said, "Go home, dear."

But I realized I couldn't go home without telling people what I had done. It was hard not to think of Andy, who had gone from a zero to a hero. I remembered how he had turned so polite and was saying Thank yous and Pleases.

So, I called out to Mrs. Tripp as she was hurrying away from the school, "Thank you, Mrs. Tripp."

I then turned to the camera and narrated what happened.

At the end, I said, "If you are watching at home, thank you, Martha, for teaching me how to throw darts."

I had left out the part about using the trick to make someone pass out. I remember Eugene saying not to tell Mom that he had taught me that. It was a good hour before we got into Mom's new Bentley and drove off. I hoped that I wouldn't get any blood on the beautiful, white leather seats.

As soon as I set foot in the house, Martha gave me a giant hug and said, "You good boy. You good boy." She was crying silently.

Mom was crying too. Eugene wrapped his arms around me and said, "Proud of you, son."

It was only noon. Even though I dreaded the number of hours before bedtime, the next few hours flew by in a blur.

There were press vans gathered outside our house as far as I could see. Just when I thought I had never known such restlessness, fear, and panic, the noise of the helicopters seeped through our roof and our walls, making me feel more of everything. The relentless whirring of the helicopters kept reminding me of what had just transpired.

Many of the neighbors were in our living room. Mom was in her element. Her only surviving child had survived a school shooting. By being a hero! She was relishing every moment of retelling my story. She didn't mind repeating it every single time, and it seemed like the neighbors didn't mind hearing and re-hearing it over and over and over again.

I was only catching bits and pieces of the talk around me. My mind would blank out ever so often. Looking back, I feel that was a good thing. It helped me detach from what was happening around me – something Professor Morrie would approve of, I thought. Seven deaths and at least 20 injured. They had rushed all the victims to the hospital. I knew the physical injuries would get everyone's attention. But what about all the cuts and wounds on the mind? Who was going to stitch up those wounds, and how?

One of the women mentioned putting up wreaths of carnations as remembrances of the killed children.

Mom thought that was a great idea.

Martha spoke up quietly, "Not good idea. A child see this wreath and it make sadness. Bring many memories. Not good idea."

Another woman said, "I recently read a book, 'The Body Keeps the Score' by Dr. Bessel Van der Kolk. Great book, by the way. Anyway, I remember one of the things he mentioned was that during disasters, young children usually take their cues from their parents."

Mom laughed nervously and said, "I failed my boy tremendously then. I just lost it at the school today and was screaming and crying my heart out when I saw Wayne walking out of the school. I was just so happy he was alive."

Martha spoke up quickly in the brief silence that followed Mom's remark. "So, if parents stay calm, everything good, yeah?"

The other woman said, "Yes. That, and make sure they take care of their children's needs. If this is done, children often survive terrible incidents without serious psychological issues."

I heard a noise at our front door and I heard a girl's voice say, "We visited Wayne when he was in the hospital. We thought he would like to see the dogs."

I stood up quickly and walked towards the front door.

"Hi, Wayne. Remember me? I'm Aditi and" pointing to a boy who was with her, the girl at the door said, "and this is Noah." Turning to the Golden Retriever who was with her, she said, "Tenzin," and pointing at me, "go say Hello."

I had seen Aditi and Noah before, when I had been in the hospital with a MRSA infection. They were middle schoolers who were also pet therapy volunteers. They were from a different school. I don't know who gave them my address. But I was really happy to see Tenzin, the Golden Retriever and Spot, the West Highland Terrier. And I didn't mind their owners too much either.

As soon as the Golden Retriever came up to me, I bent down to hug him. But then something happened that I could not control at all. I collapsed onto him and started crying my guts out. The kind of tears that would not and could not stop. At the time I did not even have enough control over my feelings to be embarrassed.

Mom later told me my whole body was shaking uncontrollably and I had a death grip on the poor dog, who made no move whatsoever to get away from me.

I cried until I could no longer feel the bone deep terror I felt back in the teacher's lounge. I still remembered the fear, but I cried till I could no longer feel it on me like another layer of skin. I took a deep breath and then I cried again when I felt this overwhelming rush of sadness for the deaths of people I didn't even get to know and would never know.

I cried for Mrs. Abramson too. I was sure no one wanted to die like that – reviled and hunted down.

It was only when Mom hugged me and said, "Let's get you upstairs and into bed, love," that I realized how exhausted I was.

I thanked Aditi and Noah for bringing their dogs, and after petting Tenzin one last time and giving Spot a quick hug, I went upstairs to my room.

When I was done showering, I realized I was too wired to sleep. I changed into a fresh pair of jeans and a tee shirt, and went back downstairs.

All the people were still gathered in our living room. The big TV trucks were still outside. The helicopters were still circling.

Eugene said it reminded him of sharks circling their victims.

I asked, "Are those police helicopters?"

Eugene smirked and said, "Nope. They are paparazzi. They want photos to sell to papers and magazines."

"Is that bad?" I asked. "Do we not want people to see what happened to us?"

"We need everyone to know what happened here, son. I don't mind that. What I don't like is their complete lack of sensitivity and grace. They don't let a community mourn. Instead, here they are, reminding us we are being watched and not letting us forget this horrific incident, even for a second." He looked out of one of our front windows and said angrily, "Preying on our pain. Vultures."

Eugene looked so upset that I immediately mimicked his tone and said, "Sharks."

Eugene smiled.

Mom said, "Everyone is so frantic with their need to know everything that goes on in the world. We all want to be the first one to break the news and social media certainly helps us do that."

I asked, "How can we break the news and still let a community mourn?"

Eugene paused in his pacing and looked thoughtfully at me.

"I don't know, son. We never had to deal with this when I was your age, or even your mom's age." He then sat next to me on the couch and said, "Maybe your generation will show us how to chase down news and still be gracious, kind, and sensitive."

"Will this change our gun laws?" Mom wanted to know.

Eugene, who owned a large collection of firearms, said, "Gun ownership is not the issue. We have to be careful who we sell the guns to and ensure that no child or mentally ill person has access to them."

I wanted to ask Eugene how we could avoid selling firearms to people who carried hate in their hearts, but I was too beat and the best I could do was to try and keep up with the conversation around me.

One of the neighbors said, "Yes, well, what about the gun shops? How do they get the license to own a gun shop? And who gets to say who can be a gun shop owner? And what about all the guns you can purchase at street corners and dark alleys?"

Mom asked angrily, "Who made guns so freely accessible?"

"It's in our constitution. Our right to bear arms," said yet another neighbor.

"There was a need for that, centuries ago when we needed to protect ourselves against a tyrannical foreign force like the one we ran from, to create this nation," said Mrs. Hollinger, who lived across the street.

One of the other neighbors asked, "What are we going to do about the parents who should have locked up their guns and didn't? Unless we hold the parents accountable, kids are going to steal these weapons from their own homes and commit these horrendous crimes. I say, we should start punishing the parents."

Mrs. Hollinger said sadly, "Don't you think they suffer enough? I don't know which is worse, to have your child murder other children and live to suffer the consequences of their crime or be arrested by police?!"

Mom cried out at that and said, "Oh, this is just way too horrible to think about." She turned towards me and asked, "Are you hungry yet, love?"

I wasn't. I hadn't eaten a bite since breakfast that morning, but I couldn't shake the image of the dead kids and dead

Mrs. Abramson. I couldn't shake the screams out of my head either.

I forced myself to smile at Mom and said, "I think I will go to bed in a bit."

"Well, let me tuck you into bed."

"Mom," I laughed – my first genuine laugh since my nightmare of a morning – "I am not a kid anymore. Besides, you have guests. I will have breakfast with you in the morning. How about that?"

Martha said, "Mrs. Humphries, I make sure Wayne is fine. You stay with guests. You chat with Mr. Humphries and guests."

When Martha walked into my room with me, my bed had already been turned down and there was a pair of Iron Man pajamas on the bed.

"I know you like 'Iron Man' movie, Wayne. I get new pajamas from store, today. I already wash for you."

I turned around and hugged Martha with all my strength. I didn't understand why someone who wasn't related to me or hadn't even known me that long would be so kind to me.

It made me want to cry. I hated that feeling.

Martha was great. She knew exactly what to say to distract me from my sadness. "Now you hero, Wayne. But hero still need to floss. Need to brush teeth." She then displayed all of her teeth and said, "You see, too much candy, not good flossing. Five root canals. Ten crowns. I am poor, but my dentist is rich." Martha laughed again.

I laughed too. I hated flossing and brushing my teeth, but didn't want my teeth to end up like Martha's – root canals and crowns.

Once I had brushed my teeth, I changed into the new pajamas and climbed into bed. I felt like a fraud wearing Iron Man pajamas. Unlike Iron Man, I had been consumed by fear, and would probably never have left the pantry if Bob hadn't forced me to.

Martha knocked on the door and came into my room again. Sitting at the edge of my bed, she said, "You see and hear rough things today, Wayne. But now, you safe. I am proud of you. So proud. Today, YOU make choice to be out of comfort zone. Today, YOU save the day."

I managed to give her a smile. How do you tell anyone at all that your first instinct had been to hide? That the only reason you got out of that cleaning closet was because Bob had OCD and knew the position of the door had shifted! And once I got out of that closet, I really had to keep going and hunt the other two shooters down or risk being shot to death. How do you confess that it wasn't your love of your classmates or your heroic nature, but rather a deep terror of being gunned down that had you "saving the day"?

I took my diary out that night and stared at it for a while. Although terrified of letting my thoughts loose, I couldn't stop writing once I had started.

Dear Tommy,

I didn't know any of the dead except for Krish. In the brief moments I knew him, Krish had shown himself to be an interesting, fun, curious, and extremely smart kid. I have a feeling we just lost someone who could have gone on to cure cancer or reverse blindness or invent something we wouldn't be able to live without.

Life doesn't make sense to me. All our lives we are told we need to behave, we need to go to school, stay off the streets. And yet, children are dying in schools. And they are being killed by other children! I know I ~~am~~ was a bully, but I never, not even when I was the angriest I have ever been, wanted to kill anyone.

Why are these children killing other children? And why is it that in this age of transparency where our clicks on the internet generate so much data, we are still unable to detect these massacres being planned? Even though I am only 14, I know we are not doing something right.

I was so scared, Tommy. Is that what children in Yemen or Syria or any of the other countries at war, feel?

My chest hurts. When I first heard the shouting and the screaming, Tommy, my heart shattered into pieces. There was so much fear and pain in those screams.

I have to...I must...make a promise to all those who died today. From this moment on, I take a breath not just for me, but for all those I could not save.

Anything can happen at any moment. If something happened to Mom, I would just die. But if something were to happen to me, I know Mom would go crazy. How will all the parents whose children died today, go on? When Marcy died, Mom had me.

Tommy, I am really sad today. Does God exist? Will he help all these parents? Mom and I never talked about God, but I think I would like to say a prayer. God, please be kind to all the families who lost a child or family member, today. Death is so sad and it is so final. You cannot go to a hospital and cure dying. Please give all these families something that chases their fears, their tears, their helplessness, their feelings of desperation. Please help them. Please, dear God. And if you exist, is there any way you can visit them and leave signs so they know you visited them?

One more thing, Tommy. I started the day in school by reminding myself to write down my goals and my strategies for those goals. Here goes:

My goals	My strategies
To not bully anymore.	Don't hurt or insult anyone. It doesn't matter how – words, objects, or behavior. Be kind. Use kind words and kind behavior.
To make friends.	Listen when others talk to me. Smile at people. Try not to hurt anyone in any way. Help people if I can. Be happy when something good happens to somebody else.
To pay attention in school.	Raise my hand in class and ask questions, even if they are stupid questions. That will force me to pay attention to what the teacher is saying.

To pay it forward. (I think I did that very well today.)	Do something for others that will make their lives better.
To be nice.	Help others.
Something has to change. I can no longer be the person who stabbed Andy with a pencil.	I need that to be my motto. Something has to change. I need to remind myself of that, every single day. Make small changes, every single day.

I am too tired to write anymore, Tommy. I will write again, later.
Wayne.

CHAPTER 10
THE AFTERMATH

I could not sleep that night. Every time I closed my eyes, I heard screams and sounds of crying. I heard the shooters laughing about killing Mrs. Abramson.

When last counted, there were seven deaths. I knew it could have been worse. I knew that. I started shivering violently when I thought of what might have happened if I hadn't been bored in Miss Samuels's class. If I hadn't asked to take a bathroom break. If I hadn't warned Brock and Maisy. If the active shooter alarm had gone off later than it had. I tossed and turned the entire night. I could not stop the crazy circus that was going on in my head.

As the sun was coming up and my room started to fill with the soft light of dawn, I got out of bed. I had not slept at all. I went downstairs and into the backyard so I could practice throwing darts. My throwing arm was bandaged. I thought it would be the perfect time to learn to throw with my left arm.

I jumped out of my skin when I felt a hand on my back.

It was Eugene. "Sorry, son. I didn't mean to startle you."

I just smiled and kept throwing darts. I never made bull's eye or even hit the board.

"Listen, son, I am sure there won't be school for the rest of the week. Shall we go sailing?"

I shrugged. I didn't care.

Mom joined us in the backyard. Eugene mentioned sailing, and my Mom said, "Oh, that would be nice. But maybe the school or the cops want to talk to Wayne. Maybe we should stick around for a day or two."

Eugene said, "They can all wait. This kid comes first."

That did it. I am embarrassed to say I burst into tears. Not the kind of tears where you make ugly faces as you try to suppress the crying, but the loud, primitive, uncontrolled kind of tears I had shed the day before. It was ugly. Mom and Eugene rushed towards me and held me. It felt like I was crying out my fears, my shame, my regrets, and my sadness. Again.

When I was done, Mom brushed the hair away from my face and asked gently, "Would you like some breakfast, love?"

Crying those tears made me feel a little dead. I don't know how else to explain it. I had caught bits and pieces of conversations last night and knew three kids my age were dead. I could not bear the thought of food. However, I was really grateful that the crying had exhausted me so much I could barely keep my eyes open.

"Mom, I would like to go to bed."

When I woke up, my room was dark and the curtains at my window were drawn. I had no idea what time it was. I saw a movement and realized it was Martha sitting in a corner of my room.

As soon as she saw me move, she came up to the bed and asked, "How you feel, kid?"

I didn't feel refreshed or good. I felt this tremendous weight all the way from the middle of my chest to the top of my nose. It was a little hard to breathe.

I asked, "What time is it?"

"It's 7:00 in the evening, Wayne. I change your dressing. You healing good."

I had slept for a good 12 hours. I hadn't even heard Martha or felt her changing my dressing. My arm ached. My head hurt. On a misery scale of one to ten, I was at a 20. But I wasn't going to complain. I was alive, after all – not something I could share with the seven others who, like me, had started out alive yesterday!

"Drink this juice now," Martha said. "It make you feel good. Then you shower, and I get you dinner and Tylenol."

I drank the juice she gave me – some concoction of coconut water, fruits, aloe vera for healing, turmeric to counter any inflammation, and black pepper to help absorb the turmeric, Martha said.

The same as yesterday, our entire downstairs was occupied by what looked like everyone from our street.

I caught snippets of the same conversations. In some weird way, I felt relieved to know that I was not the only one going in circles.

I had just finished dinner in Eugene's private den and had taken some Tylenol, when Mom and Eugene walked in with a young woman.

"Son, this is Mrs. Partyka," Mom said. "She is a counselor and would like to just speak to you about what happened at the school yesterday."

I really didn't want to talk about it. Eugene seemed to know what I was thinking because he said quickly, "Just have a conversation, son. Nothing urgent. Not even necessary for you to talk, really. But she knows something about darts too, and I thought that might interest you."

Eugene was right. That did interest me.

"Hi Wayne," Mrs. Partyka extended her hand towards me and asked, "So, I hear that you are training to compete at dart throwing."

"Yes," I said tiredly.

"I also hear that you used your skills to take down a shooter yesterday."

"Yes," I answered hesitantly.

"Were you scared?"

I didn't care for that question. Of course, I was scared. What did she expect me to say?

After a few minutes of silence, she said, "I know that was a dumb question to ask. I asked you that so you would feel something other than the terror or sadness of yesterday."

I looked up at her and she smiled. She had kind eyes, intelligent eyes. They seemed to look straight into me. Do you know what I mean?

"You can talk to me as long as you want, or not at all. But know that I am here and my job is to make you feel less afraid. My job is to make you feel that you will be okay no matter what experiences you are going through."

After saying that, Mrs. Partyka waited. Silently.

Eventually, I said, "If I had stopped to think about it, I would not have left the teacher's lounge."

When I didn't say anything else, Mrs. Partyka asked me, "What made you leave the lounge?"

"I don't know. It would be nice if I could say I knew it was up to me to save the day or that it was up to me to take the shooters down. But I didn't know anything. I mean, I really didn't know anything at all. I was not prepared for any of it. Not the actual incident. Not the fear. I had to force myself to not think of the fear. And I did something then which I kind of already knew I am really good at. I focused. I focused on me. And I did that by imagining I was someone else who was pretending to be me. That way, I was another person seeing my body tying up Bob, and then taking down Mel, and then going in search of Jamie."

Mrs. Partyka leaned forward and asked, "Do you know what that's called, Wayne?"

I nodded my head and said, "Out-of-body experience."

She said, "You're right. Intense fear of death can cause an out-of-body experience to happen. It's as if you were melted in your own personal crucible. Who you are now is a concentrated version of who you used to be, Wayne. Life will never be the same for you. And that is a good thing. Don't get me wrong. The loss of your classmates or teachers is something you should never have experienced. And I am deeply sorry that you did. I am also sitting here realizing I am talking to a 14-year-old who saved lives just yesterday, and all because he learned to throw darts really well over the summer, and because he had a desire to help. You are a brave young man and I am intensely proud of you."

I was sitting there listening to Mrs. Partyka when I heard the jerky, choppy sounds of a helicopter and the memories came rushing back.

My heart started racing, my hands became clammy, and I started shivering. It was hard to breathe. I felt as if I was breathing through a pillow held to my face – I had to really drag the air into my lungs. My brain erupted with hundreds of thoughts, all at once.

I was terrified I was losing my mind. I clung to my sanity with all my focus, my will power. One second at a time. One moment at a time. One breath at a time.

Mrs. Partyka was kind. She immediately got up and sat next to me on the couch. She had her arms around me and said, "I got you. You're home now. We got you."

I honestly cannot tell you how long we sat there.

I knew when I was almost back to normal again because my breathing became normal instead of rough.

"You okay?" asked Mrs. Partyka.

When I nodded, she got up and sat across from me again.

She looked at me with her kind eyes and asked, "Do you want to talk about it?"

I looked at her and said, "That came out of nowhere."

"The helicopter sounds magnified your memories, I think. It is what it is, Wayne. We will work through this together, okay?" Mrs. Partyka said gently.

Over the next few days, or were they weeks – time no longer felt the same – my emotions came at me in waves. There were times when I felt normal. When I was practicing darts, even if it was with my left arm or when I was speaking to Martha or being around Mom and Eugene at the same time. But then, I would hear a helicopter or catch the snippet of a conversation that invariably mentioned the incident, and my heart would start palpitating and I would have to focus really hard on my breathing. If I didn't, I felt like I was back in school, stuck in the cleaning closet in the teacher's lounge.

Eugene said that was PTSD – post traumatic stress disorder. I wondered what the other children were experiencing.

We didn't go sailing, after all. I got counseling, instead.

Mrs. Partyka, who visited me every single day, said, "Don't resist any of your feelings, dear. Tell me what anchors you to the present."

I didn't even have to think about that one. I said, "Martha's voice. She is always so calm. Mom gets anxious if I get anxious. I have to work extra hard to hide my emotions from her. That makes it harder for me to deal with the whole thing."

Mrs. Partyka started saying something, but I said quickly, "One more thing. I read the book 'Tuesdays with Morrie' this summer. A line from the book snaps me out of this terror that creeps up on me, and instead, makes me feel fierce."

There was a brief silence. I didn't realize Mrs. Partyka was waiting for me to share that line with her. She asked with a smile, "Well, are you going to tell me which line it is?"

I smiled back at her. I was already feeling much better. I said, "Do I wither up and disappear or do I make the best of my time left?"

CHAPTER 11
NOT ONE MORE SCHOOL

School was closed for two weeks. I had not realized before that time could both stand still and rush by in a blur as if it was all the same. If it weren't for daylight and the lights inside the house, I would not have been able to tell if it was day or night. If it was a weekday or weekend.

I did not know any of the school kids who stopped by. Maisy did not come. I later found out she was grieving her heart out because Krish had died in the shooting. Apparently, she had a huge crush on him.

I had a steady stream of visitors. Teachers. Students. Some sincerely wanted to thank me. Some just wanted to take a picture with me for their social media pages.

My school Principal, Mrs. Dempsey, stopped by and said, "From the bottom of my heart, I say thank you, young man." She then gave me a big hug. Right before she left, she said softly so no one else could hear, "I have to remind you that darts in school can get you expelled."

I could understand why. Darts could become weapons too. I nodded at Mrs. Dempsey, anxious to convey to her that I would not do anything I was not supposed to.

The Mayor stopped by. The school superintendent stopped by. The good thing about all these people stopping by was that it kept me busy. The bad thing about all these people stopping by was that it stopped me from being natural. I felt I had to be a certain somber way in honor of those who had died in the shooting. So, each time someone stopped by, it reminded me of what had happened. Even on the rare occasion that I may have forgotten about the shooting, the visitors reminded me of it with their sad looks, whispered conversations, and words of apology. It didn't matter if they were sincere or not, those visits always made me remember those moments of terror on my first day at my new school.

Eugene was disappointed with quite a few of our visitors. He called them "titles without any real leadership skills."

He was especially angry about the Mayor's visit, whose people must have taken about 30 photos of the Mayor with me. Eugene later said if they had told him the photo was to show everyone the face of a hero, he would have been pleasantly surprised and happy. Instead they had said, "It would be nice to show the community that the Mayor is grateful for what Wayne did."

Dan and Amanda, two kids from my school, had started visiting me. It wasn't until the third day of their visit when Dan's sister, Moira, joined us that we actually started to chat and eventually, really connect with each other. Moira also went to our school and was now a high school senior.

Moira asked, "How come you are not giving TV interviews other than the one you gave to ABC immediately after the shooting?"

I really didn't have an answer. So, I asked, "Do you think I should?"

Dan said, "Yes. Who, if not you?"

"Wayne," Moira leaned forward and said, "it is important for the world to see that children our age have great ideas and opinions. We are the ones who are going to have to step up and save the day."

Amanda said, "If it were me, I would give interviews. From the fame I get, I would try to have my own show on TV."

Moira laughed at that and said, "Really? Do you want to be a reality star?"

Amanda said, "Of course. Do you not see how rich the Kardashians are? I want my own private jet and tons of jewelry, and when I am old, my own plastic surgeon, of course."

Moira said angrily, "We are school children. We should not be thinking about all this. We should not be having two weeks off because some of us tried to kill all of us."

Amanda asked, "We are not the first school to go through this, Moira. This will happen again. Another school will go through this."

"NO," Moira exclaimed angrily. "Not one more school. WE HAVE TO SPEAK UP. YOU," Moira turned towards me and said, "YOU have a tremendous opportunity to be heard, to be our voice, to speak to people who for the only time ever may actually give you a minute of their time. YOU have to say something. Give interviews. Do something. IF YOU DON'T," Moira sat down before continuing in a softer voice, "you are just as culpable as the next school shooter."

I had not expected that.

I looked at Dan and Amanda, and asked, "Why are you here?"

When they both looked shocked, I said quickly, "I don't mean it as an insult. I really want to know what makes you come over and sit with me every day."

Amanda was the first to speak. She said, "You are new to our school. You didn't know anyone and yet you decided to save all of us. You could have hidden inside that closet and the shooters would have never found you out."

As soon as Amanda stopped, Dan said, "Why did you decide to save us?"

Much as I wanted to be honest with them, I mean really honest with them, I did not have the courage to tell them my real reason for tackling the shooters – that if I hadn't done that, the shooters would have killed me for sure.

To change the topic, I asked, "Who is the bully at our school?"

Amanda, Moira, and Dan looked at each other before Amanda said, "We have some aggressive personalities, but no one who is a bully."

I was shocked to hear that. I didn't think there were schools that didn't have at least one bully.

"How is that even possible? I asked.

Moira said, "Our school philosophy is that bullies don't develop overnight. A bully starts small and when he gets away with that, he goes onto the next slightly bigger step and so on until he is an overt bully."

That was very similar to my own experience. But I said nothing. I didn't want my new school to know that I used to be a bully.

Moira asked me, "Why did you ask about school bullies?"

I wanted to reply with, "*What if a school bully had saved you all?*" I wanted to know their answer to that question. But I was afraid of giving myself away if I said that. Instead, I asked, "I was only wondering if Bob, Mel, and Jamie had been bullied."

"They were not bullied at our school," said Dan.

"I am shocked that Jamie was one of the shooters," said Amanda. "He was always so polite to everyone, especially to Mrs. Abramson."

There was a moment of silence while we all remembered poor Mrs. Abramson and the other victims. We all had tears in our eyes.

Thinking to distract everyone, I asked, "How do you set up something so there are no bullies at the school?"

"If any of the kids show aggression, we have a team of teachers who talk to them. Our teachers constantly remind us to communicate with them," said Moira.

"Yes, but what if the other kids find out and make fun of you or worse, bully you even more?" I asked. *I knew that is exactly what I would have done as a bully who had been tattled on.*

"That's why it's a team of teachers who address the problem," said Moira, patiently. "They keep a close eye on the students involved and they follow up."

Amanda said, "Our teachers take this very seriously, Wayne, you'll see. They remind us regularly to communicate with them, to tell them of any problems."

Moira said, "Our teachers do their best to motivate us instead of brow-beating us. They try to see what we have natural aptitude for instead of trying to force us to learn something. For instance, I am really good at Math. So, they put me in a class where I get advanced Math and a lot of praise and recognition for it. I ride that wave of self-confidence at the beginning of each day and carry that over into my weakest class and then slowly build my strength there as well."

Dan piped up, "Our teachers encourage a little progress every day, even on weekends. We spend at least an hour every Saturday and Sunday on our strongest subject followed immediately by an hour on our weakest subject."

I made a face.

Moira saw me and laughed. She said, "Believe me, two hours out of the 14 or 15 hours you are awake is not a bad investment for your future."

Amanda said, "I am in your class, Wayne. You saw how Mrs. Tripp and Mr. Laboy started their lectures. All the teachers do that. They start by first inspiring us. They make us laugh. They tell us WHY we are learning something."

I was now really confused and shocked that this kind of a school had experienced an active shooting.

"I haven't watched the news. Do you know why these three did what they did?" I asked all three of my classmates.

Moira spoke up first. "They are talking about deep, mental illness." Looking at Dan, she said, "Our dad is a psychiatrist and he said, it doesn't take special skills to see that all three of them are mentally ill."

Amanda asked, "Would things have been different if they had been diagnosed?"

I asked, "Is mental illness curable?"

Moira said, "It depends. My dad would say they are manageable. Kind of like diabetes or arthritis. You can manage mental illness with counseling sessions, with proper medication, and with a support system that recognizes when you are going off the deep end and helps you get back on track."

"Are you saying that these three would not have done what they did if they had been diagnosed and treated?" I asked.

Moira said, "Yup. Pretty much. But don't forget the support system. We need to consider that to be almost just as important. That's what my dad thinks and he is the smartest man I know."

Amanda said, "With past school shootings, the shooter also killed himself. Thanks to you, Wayne, we were able to capture Bob, Mel, and Jamie. The problem is no one knows what to do with them."

Moira said, "I would be very surprised if any one of you could name all seven who died. In the meantime, everyone is talking about Bob, Mel, and Jamie. All the news channels, social media, our parents, teachers, all of us here and everywhere else, are talking about the shooters and calling them by name! And guess what? We are wholeheartedly fulfilling their desire for glory!" Looking at each one of us in turn, Moira asked, "Did you know school shooters fell into two categories?" She held up the thumb on her right hand and said, "Those who seek glory for their heinous crime," and holding up her right forefinger, she continued, "and those who are suicidal and see themselves dying as they commit a heinous crime against those they hate."

In the brief silence that followed, I started speaking. "Krish, Mrs. Abramson, Dan, Stacy, Belinda, Jeffrey, and Andrew."

The names of those who died on that ill-fated, first day of school.

For some reason that made Moira cry.

Luckily for us, Martha walked in just then, with a tray of freshly baked chocolate chip cookies. Setting the tray down, she asked, "What you think should happen now? You think these 14-year-olds should take death penalty?"

Dan said, "Yes. They were smart enough to plan this. If you can plan something so horrific and actually carry it out and not show remorse afterwards – I don't know what we can call it. Yes, they should die."

Amanda said, "We can't do that. We are not animals. We can't kill children. We shouldn't be sending **children** to be killed."

Dan asked, "Why not? Happens in all the developing countries in the world. Look at any of the countries where there's civil war."

Moira said, "You are both right. Dan, yes, children are dying or being killed every day, even right now as we sit here eating the best chocolate chip cookies I have ever had in my life. Thank you, Martha."

Martha just smiled and said nothing.

Moira continued, "But these children are dying in countries where there are so many other problems that there is a breakdown in values. Malnutrition. Lack of access to healthcare. Lack of education. Extreme poverty. Corruption. Famine." Moira was ticking off these names on her fingers. "We all know that children should always be protected and not hunted down or prosecuted for crimes that our society conditions them to commit."

I asked, "So, these three boys, do you think they should be protected?"

Moira said, "Maybe protected is the wrong word. They should certainly receive treatment for their mental illness."

Martha asked, "Who pay for treatment?"

Moira said, "Insurance does, if and when applicable. The family does if they can afford to and if insurance won't cover the cost. And if the shooter is on welfare, well then, the state does."

Martha asked, "Who pay state to pay for treatment?"

Moira said, "Tax dollars."

Amanda said softly, "So if the families of the shooters cannot afford to pay for treatment, the parents of the children who died will be paying for treatment. Mrs. Abramson will also have contributed to paying for treatment, right?"

Moira nodded. "I know. It doesn't seem fair. Then again, in a way it is fair because we created a setup which, in turn, created this scenario. Whether we want to believe it or not, we are all responsible for what happens around us. And we pay for it one way or another. We either pay for it initially by making the effort and giving our love and attention or we pay for it afterwards by being victims to the circumstance. I say we step up and decide to pay for each other with our kindness, and love, and attention, and support. That way, no one is undiagnosed, and everyone has a support system."

"Is this even possible?" I asked. "People move all the time. It is hard to immediately develop a support system when you are in a new place." I knew this from my own experience.

Martha spoke up again and said, "In my country, neighbors keep eye out for neighbors. Even if you new neighbor. No baby sitter needed. You want to go out, no problem. You ask neighbor to watch your kid. If kid get in trouble or do bad things, there are many mothers in the neighborhood who know. They yell. They fix problem. People know what other people are doing. But important is people know other people very well. Very important, we care for each other and help each other."

Moira raised her hand as if she was in class and wanted to ask a question. When Martha nodded at her, she said, "Martha, I think what you have described doesn't exist in mainstream America. Here we are pretty happy if people don't bother us. If a bunch of women intervened when a kid misbehaved, I am pretty sure no one would appreciate it. Those women would be called interfering or worse."

Amanda nodded her head and said, "Yes, I agree. I know my parents don't like it when I invite friends over who are not in 'our social class' and who don't belong to our circle of friends."

Moira laughed and said, "You mean your social class of surgeons and litigation attorneys?"

Amanda said, "And those who are members of our club."

"What club?" I asked, naively.

Moira said, "She means our country club. Eugene is a member. I'm sure we will see you there soon."

Martha asked again, "What about three shooters? In your school of no bullies, no one see them have warning sign of mental illness, yeah?"

"That is an excellent question, Martha," Moira said. "Bob had OCD."

When Amanda started saying something, Moira held up her hand and said, "Although OCD is a mental illness, my dad says people with OCD are no more likely to shoot people than the rest of us who are not OCD. But my dad also said that Jamie sounds like he is a psychopath. That's the kid who was super nice and sweet to everyone and yet he was the one who shot Mrs. Abramson so heartlessly."

"I wonder if his parents knew about his diagnosis?" Although Amanda was the one who asked the question, I was also very curious to know the answer.

Moira said, "Word in the club is that Jamie had been on treatment for his mental illness. None of these kids had ever really been in trouble for anything. And no one has a clue about Mel's mental status."

"How did they all meet?" I asked.

"Their parents are very good friends. You know," Dan looked at Moira and Amanda before continuing, "all of us

116

have been in the same school since kindergarten. None of us saw any suspicious behavior."

Martha shook her head and said, "It is very sad when your child become killer." Martha had a solitary tear running down her left cheek as she said, "How you ever recover from that? You hate them, and at same time you keep on loving them."

"I wonder if the parents ever feel guilty," I said.

Amanda said, "They must, right? And how could you ever get over it? What if they had seen the warning signs? What if they had called the cops and reported their child?"

Eugene who had just walked into the room said, "Remember, with the red flag law, you also need to show evidence that the person you are reporting is an actual threat. If there is evidence of an attempt to kill or the person is in possession of explosives, they are now looking at jail time."

"But because of our judicial system, we also follow due process, right?" Moira sounded angry, as she continued, "We also give criminals..."

"Aren't they would-be criminals before the due process happens?" Amanda boldly interrupted Moira.

"Yes, yes, you're absolutely right, Amanda," Moira said with a wave of her hand. "We also give would-be criminals their right to fair, legal representation in court."

When there was silence, my mind was racing and I started speaking before I could clam up and get shy. "About a month or so ago, Eugene and I were talking about how we can do more than what the red flag law does."

I turned to look at Eugene and asked, "Remember?"

Eugene smiled at me and said, "Yes, I remember. Do you? Can you tell your friends what we talked about?"

I racked my brain to try and remember. I knew it was a long conversation.

I finally blurted out, "You said everyone should have access to great mental health care."

When I looked over at Eugene, he was smiling and nodding as if there was more that I needed to remember. I didn't. I spoke up again to try and cover up the fact that I couldn't recall everything we had talked about. "But how do you make someone get that mental health care? And shouldn't we also be thinking about how to prevent someone from wanting to kill others? I mean, isn't there a way to find out who the would-be killers are, sooner rather than later?"

"I know, I know, I know what we should do to prevent all this," Amanda said excitedly. "We should make every child, no, wait, we should make everyone go through a mental health screening. We should do this regularly."

"Bad idea," said Moira. "I guarantee you many of us will receive some kind of a mental health diagnosis."

"Really?" I asked. "So, are we all walking time bombs?"

"I think so," Moira said, sounding nervous.

Eugene said slowly, "If all of us got some kind of a mental diagnosis, it would make mental illness more kosher. People would be okay with receiving one such diagnosis because Dan, Amanda, Moira, Martha, Eugene, and Wayne have also received such a diagnosis. And if we operate on the premise that we are all walking time bombs then we might, just possibly, treat each other with more kindness and more sensitivity."

"That's brilliant, Eugene," Moira said with excitement. "I have to tell my dad what you just said. He will probably call you to chat about all this."

Eugene smiled and said, "Anytime."

"I don't know about you all, but I want to become a psychologist or a psychiatrist when I grow up," Amanda said with a smile.

"Well, you'll never want for patients, that's for sure," Moira said. She laughed abruptly before continuing, "Especially if you push for regular mental health screenings for all children. Amanda, didn't you just say you want to be a reality star? Like the Kardashians?"

"Why can't I do both? I can have a show where I solve problems on air," Amanda said with a laugh.

Moira laughed too and looking at me, she asked, "Wayne, do you know our school has set up counselors in the gym room? Both counselors and therapy dogs have been visiting, making sure that all the kids have access to both."

I didn't know that, but before I could say anything, Amanda asked, "Have you talked to any of the counselors?"

I shrugged, unsure whether I wanted anyone else to know that I was speaking with Mrs. Partyka. It was difficult for me to open up to her and it was even more difficult for me to open up to kids my age.

I had never had friends before and wasn't really sure how much to tell them.

What if I said too much and it disgusted them? It felt so nice to have their company and their enthusiasm around me. What if I got used to it and then all of a sudden, I said the wrong thing and they decided to stop talking to me?

Amanda spoke up in the brief silence that followed my shrug. "It is difficult to open up to someone you've only just met."

Moira laughed and said, "Not for you. You are one of the most outgoing people on the planet."

Amanda said, "No, seriously. I spoke to a counselor and it was difficult. I have no idea why!"

Eugene patted Amanda on her back and said gently, "Because the consequences of what you say now are different. You all just went through a life-altering event, and you are expected to talk about it to a person you had never met before. Part of your healing process, but still very hard."

"Would it have helped if you had some kind of a contact with the counselor previously?" Moira asked, getting up and sitting next to Amanda.

"Maybe. I don't know," said Amanda. "I mean, I know our school has counselors. But I've heard that they are too busy to offer counseling. I heard one of the kids say that her sister, Melanie, went to see a counselor and got shooed out of the office because the counselor was busy doing some scheduling work. When she went back another time, she couldn't even find the counselor. Someone said she was busy in the cafeteria, making sure the kids were behaving! And after she went back a third time and the counselor was about to go on bus duty, Melanie never went back."

Moira shook her head and said, "That's really bad. Our dad says counselors play a crucial role in schools and should not be distracted from their duties. They have a critical job to train and guide young minds to be healthy, happy, and productive. He says kids spend so much time in schools that we have to get them the best teachers and counselors in schools."

"I agree with that philosophy," Eugene said, before adding, "Schools are their own ecosystem, where, in addition to education, kids can, and should learn how to be kind, how to work with other kids, how to cheer for each other, and how to be happy. Any school that can do that will create future leaders."

Moira smiled at Eugene and said, "I really like that."

Eugene smiled back at Moira and then, turning towards Amanda, he said, "I like what you said, earlier, kid. You said that all of us should receive regular mental health screenings. I think we should add regular counseling sessions, too. Imagine having a person you already know, helping you through a crisis such as this. Their ability to help you, and your own ability to accept that help and to accelerate that help, will be tremendous. You will no longer be so hesitant to tell these professionals your deepest fears."

Moira said, "My dad says writing about the traumatic experience, your own feelings about it, and the impact you think the traumatic event is having on your life, is a great way to get going with recovery."

"Wasn't Jamie on medication?" Amanda asked Moira.

"Yes, he was," Moira replied. "My dad thinks he must have stopped taking them."

"What good is a diagnosis if we cannot be sure the patient gets treated?" Amanda asked angrily, before continuing, "And who takes responsibility for that? If a psychopath is off his medicine and commits a crime, who is responsible for that crime?"

"Amanda, are you saying that Jamie's parents are responsible for his crime?" Moira asked, sounding very surprised.

"No, of course not. Well, I don't know. Maybe, they are responsible. Everyone at the club is saying that Jamie stole the guns from his parents. Shouldn't they have locked their guns away, especially when they knew Jamie was mentally ill?" asked Amanda, sadly.

Dan said, "My parents know Jamie's parents very well. They are both responsible people. So, the suspicion is that Jamie broke into his parents' safe to get the guns out."

Martha looked around at us and said, "There has to be solution to this. Something simple and we don't see yet."

No one said anything for a few minutes. Thinking simple was not that easy.

Finally, Moira said, "Although this not the case for our school, other school shooters were often overheard planning their carnage or had left social media messages about their plans and yet, no one reported them! What if someone had? I think schools need to teach all children that it is okay to report the presence of weapons on campus and that they really MUST report not only the presence of weapons, but also all threats of violence."

Eugene said, "We have a program called 'Fortify Florida,' right here in Florida. There is an App you can download on your smart device or people can go online to 'getfortifyfl.com' and report any suspicious activity anonymously."

"That way, you remove the fear of retaliation," I said and smiled, when Eugene patted me on the back.

Dan cleared his throat and said, "All the school shooters so far have been mentally ill. However, not all mass shooters are mentally ill. Instead, they act out a hate-based ideology. Our mom" Dan looked at me and continued, "is a social scientist and she read an article to us yesterday that talked about mental illness only contributing to about 3 percent of violent crime in America. So, these mental health screenings we are talking about are not going to prevent hate crimes. What can we do to prevent hate crimes?"

None of us knew the answer to that, but our discussion would have to wait. My visitors had to leave for an appointment with school counselors.

CHAPTER 12
SOMETHING HAS TO CHANGE

We walked over to Maisy's house the day after Moira, Amanda, and Dan had that intense discussion with me.

Maisy's housekeeper opened the door. She smiled at us and said, "Amanda, nice seeing you. Come in. Come in."

We looked at each other and let Amanda take the lead. She smiled and said, "Good morning, Aida. Will you please take us to Maisy?"

Aida led us up the stairs and down a hallway where she opened the door to a room without even knocking on it.

The room was dark. That was the first thing I noticed. It was gigantic. That was the second thing I noticed. Maisy was still in bed and was trying to sit up – that was the third thing I noticed. Aida walked over to the window and drew the curtains. The fourth thing I noticed was a huge black and white photograph of Krish that took up almost an entire wall. He was laughing at something. He looked so happy and vibrant. So alive. We all gasped.

While the others went up to the bed and towards Maisy, I went back outside and sat down on the floor in the hallway. I put my head in my hands and just focused on breathing, which I was having a really hard time doing.

Dan found me there. Holding me by the arm, he quickly walked me home. We lived down the street and around the corner from Maisy's.

Martha opened the door and after a short, whispered conversation with Dan, she gave me an enormous hug and walked me to the kitchen. I sat at a table while she baked cookies. When the doorbell rang, Martha said, "Come with me, dear."

When Martha opened the door and I saw it was Mrs. Partyka, I am embarrassed to say I started crying.

Mrs. Partyka hugged me and walked me into the den. Once we took our usual spots, she asked gently, "What are you feeling in this moment?"

I said, "Guilty."

Mrs. Partyka asked, "What inside you feels this way?"

Although Mrs. Partyka had asked me the same question before, this was the first time I wanted to answer her. I wanted her to help me. Desperately.

I could still see the image of Krish so very clearly – the one holding up my dart. I could not bear the thought that I might have been able to save him and didn't.

Right then, the door opened and Mom ran towards me. As soon as she reached me, she burst into tears and started hugging and kissing me.

Although I was happy to see Mom, I started having trouble with my breathing again. That was too bad. I had just started to feel like I could breathe without panicking.

As soon as Mom calmed down a little, Mrs. Partyka said kindly, "Would you like to stay for the session?"

Mom said tearfully, "Oh yes, please, thank you so much."

Mrs. Partyka said gently, "Welcome to our space. What I am doing right now is called Internal Family Systems therapy. This means we consider the mind to be made up of parts, like members of a family. My goal is to ensure that all these parts get along. These different parts of the mind can help each other, but each part can still have experiences that the other parts never know about. These different parts have their own abilities and needs. We have to make sure to approach these different parts with curiosity, interest, and compassion. I want Wayne to dig out that part of his mind that is confident, curious, and calm. And believe me when I say that there exists such a part in each and every one of us. We just have to do a little digging, and like I said before, we have to dig with curiosity and compassion."

Mom just nodded her head repeatedly.

I think she was too afraid to say anything at all and be asked to leave the room. When Mom and I had both calmed down, Mrs. Partyka looked at me and asked again, "Wayne, you said you feel guilty. What inside you feels guilty?"

As she asked this, I saw an image of me cowering in a corner and hiding my face in my hands. When I told her what I'd seen, she asked, "How do you feel towards that boy cowering in the corner?"

According to Mrs. Partyka, this mindful separation between me as an observer and the part inside my mind that is the cowering boy is tremendously helpful in recovering from trauma.

I said, "I hate him. He disgusts me. He should have acted sooner. Krish may have been alive today. The others may have been alive today."

Mrs. Partyka asked, "Ask that hating part of you to please step back."

I did as she asked, and then looked up at her and nodded my head.

She then said, "Thank it for its vigilance. It has been trying to protect you."

I did as she asked and nodded in her direction again.

Mrs. Partyka said gently, "Now, please ask that cowering boy what he is feeling?"

I did. I repeated aloud what I had heard, which was, "I feel so alone and so sad."

She then asked, "How do you feel towards him now?"

I said, "Curious. I want to know why he feels so alone. Why he is so sad."

She then asked, "Will you ask the cowering boy how old he is?"

My shoulders slumped as I said, "Five."

I could feel Mom tensing up next to me. And the memories of my five-year-old self came rushing back. Mom had been so preoccupied with her own sadness and loneliness. Losing her daughter, her abusive husband, and even her mother, all in the same year. Back then, Mom used to pretty much leave me alone until I cried or got angry. I looked at Mom and I knew I could never blame her for what she had to do to cope with her terrible circumstances. Mrs. Partyka must have sensed my dilemma, for she said softly, "Just observe. Be curious. Be compassionate."

After a brief silence, she asked, "How do you feel towards that cowering boy now?"

I looked within my mind and sat up straight, saying clearly, "Compassionate."

"Do you want to tell him anything?" Mrs. Partyka asked.

I thought about it for a while before saying, "Yes. I want to tell him to not cower anymore. To not feel alone. I have Mom, and Eugene, and Martha." And then remembering Dan who had walked me home, I said, "And friends."

Mrs. Partyka smiled at me and said, "Remember, you look at all the parts of your mind with interest, curiosity, and compassion. If there is an angry part, ask him to step aside gently. If there is a fearful part, or a sad or traumatized part, look at it with compassion. Remember, we want to reach that part of YOU that is confident and calm."

I nodded and smiled for the first time since I got back from Maisy's.

Mrs. Partyka smiled back at me and said, "I have a suggestion for you, young man. I would like for you to write about your experience with the shooting as it happened. Write all your feelings about it and the emotions it triggers in you. And then write about the impact you think the shooting has had on your life. How it's changed your life."

When I nodded at Mrs. Paryka, I realized my breathing was no longer frantic. I was calm again.

When Mrs. Partyka left, I sat down and wrote to Tommy.

130

Dear Tommy,

When I ran into the teacher's lounge, I was thinking there was a good chance the shooters would find me. I cannot believe how lucky I was to have survived.

What if I hadn't met Martha? What if she hadn't taught me how to play darts? What if I hadn't read about Anne Frank and Professor Morrie? What if I hadn't decided to make the best of my time left? Would I even have taken up darts?

What if Eugene hadn't shown me how to take someone down by pressing on their neck?

So many What ifs?

What if those three shooters had been stopped before they got the weapons?

I am glad it wasn't me. I am glad I was not the shooter.

You know that I was a bully for the longest time, right? I had so much anger. What if that anger had turned me into a killer? That thought scares me. But it also makes me think there must be people out there who are feeling all this hate and it keeps on getting worse, but we are not doing anything to make the hate go away.

Seeing Mom happy (finally) has released some of my own anger, Tommy.

Being on a boat in the middle of the sea also somehow diluted that anger.

Doing the Internal Family Systems therapy with Mrs. Partyka also helped me today. For the first time in forever, I don't hate myself. And that feels really good.

I heard that the kids at my school are terrified of going back. They are scared of another shooting. I am not. I don't know why.

I don't want to focus on fear. I want to focus on solutions, Tommy. How can my school assure us that there WILL NOT be another shooting? What will they do differently?

131

The news people have been talking about having only ONE entryway into the school; having security personnel on school grounds as a deterrent; having an Xray bag check, so guns don't get smuggled into the school.

I think we have to do more than that, but I am not really sure what exactly.

Eugene and Amanda talked about mandatory mental health screenings. But do we have enough therapists to provide this service to every school?

Who will pay for it?

If we think of training teachers to recognize signs of mental illness, is it the same as training teachers to carry guns? That could be potentially disastrous.

We need simple solutions. I remember when Mom saved money for months and bought a super-efficient, really complicated vacuum cleaner. She used it for a month and then it was put away in our storage closet, because it was too much trouble to assemble and dissemble. Before we had Martha, we had a Dyson. Even I had fun using it to vacuum our old apartment. I feel our solutions need to be like that – more like Dyson – fun to implement, simple, and easy to use.

I am very sad that Mrs. Abramson is dead.

Even though I really, really like Maisy, I am sad that Krish is dead. He seemed like a cool kid.

Did Krish make the best of his time left? Did Mrs. Abramson? Will I?

I cannot shake the thought of what if someone had realized the three shooters were mentally ill? I mean, we know now that Jamie was a psychopath and that he must have stopped taking his medication. But we don't know if Bob and Mel are mentally ill. Even though I think there is no way a sane person can do what

132

they did, we still don't know for sure if they are mentally ill. Was it a hate crime? And how does one stop hate from forming in the first place?

It's sad and scary, Tommy. There must be other kids out there like Bob and Mel and Jamie. Right? Why aren't the grown-ups getting their act together? Why aren't they doing something? How many school shootings will it take for adults to wake up and say NEVER AGAIN?! Shouldn't it have been one?

So many things had to come together this year to kind of prepare me for this moment. I feel my entire life was a preparation for my one act of courage today. I am still unconvinced that it was courage, but that's what everyone else is calling it.

And because of how everything kind of led up to this one big moment, I feel the best thing I can do is to experience life.

To LIVE. I don't know how to make it make more sense, Tommy. I feel I just have to go with the flow, trust my insides, be who I am. BUT, to know what my insides are telling me, I feel I have to find that calm and confident part of me that is hidden underneath the other parts that are hateful or angry or afraid.

Tommy, what if stopping hate crimes was as simple as finding the part of you that was calm? That's all any of us would ever need to do. If we find the hateful part of our selves coming up, we politely ask it to step aside and then we look for the calm part of our selves. When I was a bully, I knew bullying was not the right thing to do. But the hate and anger inside me overwhelmed me until that was all I felt. It wasn't until I was consciously trying to improve myself that I was able to make an impact. And that is a cool feeling. To see that MY CHOICE led to something amazing.

Tommy, I wonder if Jamie, Bob, and Mel would have turned out to be shooters if they had gone through Internal Family Systems therapy.

133

It was crazy, Tommy. I felt so guilty and was so anxious, ashamed, and embarrassed before the session. But after the session, I felt calm. I felt kind. Can you believe it?

And I can do it anytime I want to. Mrs. Partyka showed me how. What if our school hires Mrs. Partyka to guide ALL the children, the teachers, AND the staff through Internal Family Systems therapy.

Imagine if everyone felt calm and kind! Would there be less violence?

What if, just once or twice a week, we begin our school day with a brief exercise in Internal Family Systems therapy? Just 20 to 30 minutes in the morning. Everyone meets in the Assembly Hall and gets guided by a therapist? What if there was a way to get people to sponsor therapy for all the schools?

It seems so easy. You keep looking at the different parts of your mind till you dig out the part that is calm and confident and curious. Doing that can only help you experience life better.

SOMETHING HAS TO CHANGE, Tommy. Maybe, it starts with a small group of people. I overheard one of our neighbors quoting Gandhi, "We must be the change we wish to see in the world." Maybe we need to first become the change we wish to see in the world, and then we can inspire others to change.

I don't have any answers, yet.

One last thing, Tommy. I remember sailing on Eugene's boat this summer and how just staring at the waves pulled away at my anger until all that remained was the rhythm of my breathing, the sound of the waves, and the bobbing of the boat. That was so calming. Kind of like what I felt after Mrs. Partyka took me through her Internal Family Systems Therapy.

Just like the purpose of water is to keep on moving, I feel my purpose is to find that calmness. Nothing bad can happen when you are in

that place. Right, Tommy? And maybe the purpose for all humans
is to find that calmness.
More later, alligator.
Wayne.

CHAPTER 13
SOLUTIONS

Dan, Amanda, and Moira were back at my house.

"How's Maisy?" I asked.

"Her therapist arrived," Amanda said softly.

Soon we were all gathered in the kitchen where Martha was now cooking lunch. Chicken Biryani, Aloo Paratha, and Paneer Tikka Masala. Indian food – my favorite food.

As soon as everyone took a seat, Moira said, "I think we are all agreed that all the school shooters so far have been mentally ill. I mean, we don't know about Bob and Mel, but they are probably also in that category. That said, what on earth can we do to actually diagnose them before they become shooters?"

Amanda leaned forward and said angrily, "Jamie already had a diagnosis. We have to do more than diagnose."

Moira got up from the kitchen table and started pacing. When she finally stopped pacing, she said excitedly, "We just need to create a process, an actual process that you follow at all times. Something like 1. you go to a mental health professional, 2. you get your diagnosis, 3. you get your treatment prescribed to you, 4. you do what's called 'directly observed therapy', if necessary, 5. your mental health office checks in with you every week, or month, or whatever set time, and talks to you as well as to someone responsible for you."

"Does everyone know what directly observed therapy is?" Eugene asked. I hadn't even seen him walk into the kitchen.

When I shook my head, Moira said, "It is when a patient takes his meds, his medication, in front of a responsible person - like a parent or a doctor or a nurse."

"That way you know they have taken their meds," Amanda said softly.

"What about situations where the doctor misses the diagnosis? Or the parents are irresponsible?" Eugene asked.

"I don't know, I'm just a kid," Moira said with a laugh.

Eugene laughed too and said, "We cannot have just one solution. We have to use a multi-pronged approach so no one misses their chance at diagnosis and treatment."

"Can we still use Moira's steps?" Dan asked.

Eugene said, "Yes, I think so. We need to add a #6, where you get regular counseling sessions with a therapist paid for by your insurance, and #7, where you join a support group."

"Actually, I have something to say," I said this quickly, happy to have something to contribute to this discussion. I then shared with them the intervention I had written about in my diary. "I really think Internal Family Systems Therapy is the answer to all this violence. Not just school shootings, but mass shootings, too."

"You just might be right, son," Eugene said. "I can't imagine that anyone who is feeling calm and kind would pick up a gun and start shooting innocent people."

"What we need to do is preventive therapy," I said with a smile.

"Brilliant idea," said Dan.

"Wow! A hero and a thinker," said Martha happily and started clapping her hands. Eugene, Moira, Dan, and Amanda joined in. I felt my face go red. I was pleased, but also embarrassed.

"Wayne," Eugene said, "I think it's great that we engage in prevention. But that is not cost-effective for everyone, right? We know your school can certainly afford to provide that service. But what about the public schools? How will they afford it? Our public schools have so many needs that mental help might be pretty low on their survival list."

"And that leaves us with the same questions," Moira said, "1. how do we stop hate from forming in the first place, and 2. how do we ensure that we get ALL mentally ill people the help they need?"

Eugene leaned forward and said, "Like I said earlier, we need a multi-pronged approach. 1. We need a way to implement mental health screenings for every single person who lives in our country. This needs to happen every single year or more frequently if there is a diagnosis. These screenings can also detect hatred and rage. 2. We need to create an effective and fail-proof support system in our schools with great teachers who receive ongoing training and testing in sensitivity and mentoring, as well as in recognizing the signs of mental illness, of hatred, and of rage."

Martha interrupted at this point and said, "3. We need community of neighbors. They watch out for each other. Maybe, we ask neighbors to have block parties every month."

Eugene laughed and said, "Block parties are great. I think we need a number 4. We all need to speak up more about mental illness, so it is less of a stigma and seen more like diabetes. We need Moira's process."

"You also said the same thing before, Moira," I said, "that we should consider mental illness like we consider diabetes. Are you saying that mental illness is a chronic condition?"

"I actually don't know about all the different diagnoses that make up mental illness. But, yes, I think once a person receives this diagnosis, they have to be vigilant for the rest of their lives." Moira sounded so grown up when she said this. "And there is absolutely nothing wrong with that. It's like a diabetic making healthy choices once they receive their diagnosis. It's the same thing with mental illness. You receive a diagnosis of a certain mental illness and you just move into a category with heightened awareness of what you need to do to stay healthy. You just have intimate knowledge of your own workings. I think it's so cool."

I loved how my new friends were making such perfect sense and coming up with ideas that I was convinced would solve this problem of not just school shootings, but all mass shootings. And who knows, maybe all kinds of violence?!

Eugene spoke up again and said, "We need to see mental wellness as something that can be fostered by a proper diet, by exercise, and by actively reducing stress."

"How can diet help mental wellness?" I was really curious to see how Eugene would answer this.

"I was blown away when I first read about this too, Wayne," Eugene said. "Do you know there is a big community of microorganisms in our intestines? This makes up our gut community of microbes – our gut microbiome. There are good communities that help our health, and bad communities that don't help us and maybe even harm us. The foods we eat either foster good or bad microbes in our guts. Research shows that our gut microbiome impacts every aspect of our health from infections to mental illness. Imagine if we can improve mental health by eating the right things."

"Or **prevent** mental illness by eating the right things," I said.

"Exactly," Eugene said. "You are beginning to have an inkling of the complexity of mental illness."

"What would you cut out from your diet?" I asked Eugene.

Eugene's response was quick. "I have already cut out meat from any animal that lived in stressed-out conditions like cages. In our house, son, we don't eat unnatural foods."

"What do you consider unnatural foods?" Moira asked.

"Okay," Eugene said. "For example, cows eat grass. They are not supposed to eat ground up bones of other animals. And yet that's what they eat! In our house we only eat meat that comes from free-range animals who eat natural diets that are free of antibiotics and hormones."

"What about all the packaged and processed foods?" Dan asked, saving me from the anxiety of having to ask this question.

I had wondered if Eugene would consider all my chips and cheese puffs to be unnatural.

But before Eugene could say anything, Moira laughed and said, "No way am I giving those up. I can't stay away from them."

"But what about your gut microbiome?" asked Dan.

Moira laughed self-consciously before saying, "It's hard to think gut microbiome when I can't even see it."

Eugene laughed and said, "Oh, they're there. Believe me. But to answer your question, Dan, I think it's bad if someone eats mostly processed foods, doesn't exercise, has a stressed-out life, and is without a supportive family or network of friends. This person is asking for problems."

"Everything in moderation," Martha said. I turned around. She had just taken out a large tray full of orange muffins. "Look at tray of muffins. If you eat all the muffins, very bad for you. You eat a few, is okay. You eat a few, and you exercise, that even better. Yeah?"

We all nodded our heads and smiled at Martha.

Remembering my diet from our pre-Eugene days, I said, "It's not cheap to have that lifestyle, you know. Organic foods cost more. Sometimes processed foods are just quick, easy, and fast."

"Everything boils down to choices. You choose between a bag of chips or a bag of carrots. Cookies or snap peas, you know?" Although Moira said this laughingly, I felt this was no joke.

Although we were never really poor, like food stamps poor, I still knew from my own experience, that sometimes junk food and fast food made me happy. And when life hadn't given me many things to be happy about, I took the happiness any way I could get it. Even if poor people could choose to cut out junk food, I didn't think they could afford to buy organic foods regularly. We certainly hadn't been pro-organic before Mom married Eugene.

I sighed and said, "The shooters are all just 14 years old. My age. What do you think is going to happen to them?"

"So what if they are only 14?" Dan asked angrily. "They still committed a heinous crime and should be tried as if fully cognizant of the impact they would have on their victims. And Wayne, you heard them laugh about killing Mrs. Abramson."

I nodded my head in agreement, but Dan's comment made me sad. We were four children sitting inside a luxurious mansion and discussing crimes committed by three other children.

To make matters worse, Moira said, "The shooters are probably in solitary confinement, away from everything they've ever known and experienced. And without their meds, and especially without the stabilizing anchor of their families, their mental illness must be in full force."

Amanda said sadly, "I feel they are victims too, a different sort of victim – more to do with circumstances and lack of a process."

Dan exclaimed angrily, "I cannot believe you just said that! Would you have said that if the shooters had been black?"

Amanda stared at Dan and said, "Absolutely! Why wouldn't I?"

"Good question, Dan," Moira said, interrupting Amanda, and whatever reply Dan had for Amanda. "Don't take offense, Amanda. He's just trying to remind all of us that race plays a big role in the perception of crime."

Looking at Dan, Moira said, "So, I have a question for you. What do you think of jihadist fighters? Do you think they know what they are doing? What about their mental state? Are we going to label them as mentally ill? And how do we gauge that?"

Remembering something Eugene had said earlier, I asked Moira, "Do you think these fighters are brainwashed?"

"Well, of course," said Moira. "They are manipulated to a place back in time and into an old battle, and they are brainwashed until the old wounds are raw and festering again in a new generation."

"Well said, young lady," Eugene said, patting Moira on the back.

Moira looked at all of us, as if to make sure we were all paying attention, before she turned back to Dan and asked, "What if the shooters had been radicalized and jihadist? Would you call them victims of their circumstance or would you call them terrorists?"

It was Dan's turn to stare, before he said carefully, "I want to say that I would say the same thing. But, deep down inside, I really don't know."

"You kids are very impressive," Eugene said. "What I do know for sure is we have to stop marginalizing people. We have to be kind, really kind to one another."

The doorbell rang then and I heard a voice I never thought to hear again.

"Hello, my name is Andy. Wayne and I used to go to the same school. Is he in?"

My heart started racing and I jumped up from my chair. But Mom had gotten to the front door first and had already started yelling, "How dare you show your face here? You get OUT of my house. Martha, throw this boy out."

I ran and threw myself on the door and said to my mom, "Mom, please stop. It's about time that you hear the real version of what happened."

When Mom started saying something, I said, "Mom, please listen to me."

We went back into the living room. Although my heart was still racing, my mind was very clear on what I had to do. Taking a deep breath, I looked at Andy. I saw how he was standing with his head held high and back straight. He gave me a slight nod and bowed his head as if to say *Thank you for finally coming clean.*

I looked at Eugene and my three new friends and realized that what I was about to do might very well destroy my reputation, my friendships, and my relationship with Eugene.

So, holding my head high and my shoulders back, I took a deep breath and said, "In my previous school, Andy and I were in the same class." I sighed and said, "I am ashamed to say I was a bully."

I heard a choking sound and looked up to see Mom pressing her hand to her mouth. She had tears flowing down her face. I looked away quickly. It hurt too much to look at her. Eugene got up quickly and sat next to her, putting his arms around her.

"I had so much anger inside me and I was so terrified of being hurt that I had resolved to hurt others before they could hurt me. Andy was the frequent recipient of my bullying ways. Once, when I tried to stab him with a pencil, he deflected that stab and I ended up stabbing myself. Unfortunately, that stab got infected with MRSA and I ended up in the hospital."

Silence.

I looked up at Andy first. He had tears in his eyes and when he saw me looking at him, he said, "Thank you."

Gathering up my fast disappearing courage, I said, "There's more. I didn't take down the shooters because I wanted to be a hero and save the day. I did it because Bob knew I was in the teacher's lounge. I had to act fast and once I started, I couldn't stop. I had to catch the other two as well."

Amanda started saying something and when I looked up, my heart sank into my toes. She looked so angry and disgusted. She started with, "How dare...?"

"Don't say it, Amanda. Stop right there," said Eugene. "Wayne, I can only imagine the tremendous courage it must have taken to not only own up to your mom and to the rest of us about Andy, but now to tell us about your reasons for taking down the three shooters!! I applaud you. Courage is not something one can assume to always have access to. Courage is conquering your fears despite knowing what could go wrong." Smiling at me, Eugene continued, "This is amazing, Wayne. I thought you a hero before. But now, I think you are a superhero. You are so much more than anyone I know. You show us how to be. And," he looked at everyone else in the room, "if others don't see you and applaud you for doing what could possibly be the most difficult thing a teenager can do," – he made a sound of disgust – "then they totally don't get the concept of kindness and everything we talked about earlier. I would call them hypocrites."

"Thank you," I said, trying hard not to cry.

Mom was crying silent tears. I could not bear to look at her anymore, so I looked at Andy. He held out his hand and said, "I came over to say you are a hero. And now, I say it with even more conviction. You are a hero and I am so glad to know you. Everyone at our school – sorry, I should say, everyone at **my** school is talking about you. Everyone is very proud of you, Wayne."

I gave Andy a big hug.

Andy hugged me back and said, "I have to go. My friend is waiting for me outside. Bye, everyone."

As Andy turned to leave, Mom got up, wiped her tears away and said in a shaky voice, "Andy, wait. I never thanked you before. I found out that you were the one who insisted that your principal should call me up to check on Wayne and his stab wound. You were the one who recognized my son's signs of a MRSA infection. I never thanked you for saving his life. Thank you, thank you, thank you."

Andy was very sweet. He went over to my mom and hugged her tight. I went over and joined in, which made both my mom and Andy laugh out loud. Andy said, "I'm so glad I saved your son's life, Ma'am."

Eugene also hugged Andy and said, "Come by anytime, kid. Thank you for stopping by to see Wayne."

When Andy left, Moira said, "That was intense. Eugene, thank you for telling us all what's what. Wayne, none of what we learned here today changes the fact that you are a hero. It's very possible that the only reason all of us are here today is because of what YOU did. So, thank you so very much."

Moira came over and gave me a hug. Dan and Amanda joined in. My second group hug of the day.

Dan and Amanda both said, "Thank you, Wayne."

I didn't know what I had expected when I had started confessing. It certainly wasn't a quick forgiveness.

Eugene said, "If you had met Wayne last year, you would've seen and known that he was a bully. Now, here he is, a hero who's saved the day. Which one is the real him?"

When my friends and Mom started protesting, Eugene said, "Please, hear me out. What this tells me more than anything else is to not categorize someone based on an isolated incident, unless it's something horrific, and who knows, maybe not even then. I feel that we have to always look at the circumstances. To definitely give a person a second chance, and of course, your school being Wayne's second chance."

Moira said slowly, "We have to look at the sum of our experiences with a person and not just one isolated incident."

"Are you saying we need to give the shooters a second chance, Eugene?" Dan asked. "They are cold blooded killers."

"No, no, that's not what I am saying," Eugene said. "Wayne's new circumstances brought out a different side of him. I think we need to always remember there's a higher side somewhere within all of us. Perhaps if one set of circumstances doesn't bring it out, another set might?"

When no one said anything, Mom said, "Dan is right. The three shooters had been planning this for a long time. In all that time, I'm sure they had plenty of time to reflect and mull over the seriousness of the crime they would commit."

"Any of you a Malcolm Gladwell fan?" Eugene asked.

What a random question, I thought to myself.

Everyone said "Yes," except for Mom, Martha and me.

Moira said, "If I could create a compelling story like he does, I would be a writer too. He is beyond amazing."

I was embarrassed that although I had a few of his books on my list of books to read, I hadn't yet read any of his works.

"Why do you ask?" I asked Eugene.

"Well, Malcolm Gladwell wrote an article for the New Yorker, way back in 2015, about school shootings," said

Eugene. "The weird thing is, school shooters don't fit any kind of pattern. There is a very important question in that essay, attributed to a sociologist, Mark Granovetter: *what explains a person or a group doing things that don't fit with who they are or what they think is right?* The example used in that essay was that of rioting. Rioting consists of a group of people engaged in destruction. Naturally, something happens to move these people away from normal behavior and towards acts of violence. I am not going to repeat the entire essay or the article. But I thought it was interesting that Granovetter saw rioting as a social process."

Amanda raised her hand and asked, "What does rioting have in common with school shooting?"

"I am so glad you asked, Amanda," Eugene said. "I confess I haven't read Granovetter's original essay, but Gladwell's article explains so incredibly well what I will do my best to not butcher. Apparently, Granovetter proposes that a riot is a social process. This means people behave in reaction to what's happening around them, but this reaction is also a response to the behavior of people around them."

"That happens all the time in our school," Amanda said.

"Some of us have strong personalities and might set the tone for how the class behaves," Moira said with a laugh.

"Seriously, doesn't social process happen all the time?" Amanda asked.

"Let Eugene finish what he's saying, Amanda," Dan interrupted gently.

Eugene continued, "Apparently, social processes have thresholds. According to Granovetter, it would take a person with a threshold of zero to start a riot. That person throws the first rock or projectile or whatever it is that rioters use, as a reaction to the slightest provocation. But not all rioters have that threshold of zero. The riot builds when people with higher thresholds also participate. For instance, a person with a threshold of one will throw a rock if someone else has already thrown a rock. A person with a threshold of two will join the rioters when there are two people throwing rocks. This goes on and on. Group interaction. That's pivotal to group behavior. And what Gladwell suggests in this incredibly well written article, is to use the Granovetterian model to explain the epidemic of school shootings. The idea is that when the Columbine school shooting took place in 1999, those shooters were the ones with a threshold of zero. They had grand plans and they publicized those plans on a website and in their homemade videos. From what I understand, school shooters with higher thresholds join this irreversible brutality after they watch these homemade videos and watch the surveillance footage from that school shooting."

"Are you saying that without access to those videos, people with higher thresholds won't be inspired to commit similar crimes?" Dan asked, sounding horrified.

"I don't know that for sure, Dan," Eugene said, sadly.

There was a brief silence and then, Moira gave a sudden laugh before continuing, "My mom is nicer to me after she hangs out with her group of close friends. My dad calls it a destressing session. Granovetter would have said my mom's threshold to be forgiving of my childish behavior is high. She hangs out with her friends and is influenced by their generosity and kindness to their own children. She comes home and models the behavior of her friends. Ergo, she is nicer to me."

"Not bad example," Martha said, joining our conversation. "Friendships are important. Type of friends, more important."

"Let's go back to the shooters for a moment," Eugene reminded us. "If we think of everything we do as a social process, can anyone tell me what we need to do to prevent future school shootings?"

"Regular mental health screenings and regular counseling sessions to remove anger and hate," said Moira.

Amanda asked, "Okay, but how will we remove the stigma of testing?"

"If everyone gets tested that will at least remove the stigma of testing. We have to train the tester to be sensitive and confidential too," said Eugene.

"Absolutely. And we have to really, really find a way to remove the stigma of a positive diagnosis too. So what if someone is mentally ill? It's just a health condition that can and should be managed with medicine, counseling, and maybe the therapy you were talking about, Wayne," said Moira.

"Internal Family Systems Therapy?" I asked.

"That's the one," said Moira with a smile. "And if this social process is a real thing, we have to create the right social process so people behave in a way we want them to."

"Whoa, isn't that a dangerous thing to do? You are talking about manipulating people! I am uncomfortable thinking about it," said Dan.

Moira leaned forward and said, "Whether we want to believe it or not, everything we do influences someone, does it not? If the way we behave deters school shooters and other types of mass shooters, why the heck should we not actively cultivate that behavior?"

"Good point," Dan said with a laugh.

Eugene, who had been pacing, finally sat down and said, "I have one last thing to add. You've all heard of the marshmallow test, right?"

"What this test?" Martha asked.

Looking around at us, Eugene said, "It was a test where children were left alone in a room with marshmallows and asked to wait before eating them. The psychologists running these tests were studying delayed gratification - why are some children able to resist the marshmallow until they are given permission to eat it? Why do others give in and find themselves unable to wait, unable to resist eating the marshmallow before receiving permission?"

"Eugene," Mom interrupted laughingly, "what does this have to do with school shootings?"

"You would fail the delayed gratification test, my love," Eugene said with a laugh.

All of us laughed, nervously at first, and then without inhibition. We all needed that release. I think we were all coiled tight, still tense from the shooting and tense from our discussion.

CHAPTER 14
THE MARSHMALLOW

When the laughter died down, Eugene said, "The psychologist who created the marshmallow test, Dr. Mischel, said that the key to doing really well in the marshmallow test is to not think about the marshmallow in the first place."

"I get it," Dan said excitedly. "For a school shooter, this would be finding ways to avoid thoughts of shooting."

"Exactly," Eugene said. "Either the would-be shooters do this themselves or the school sets up an active system of enforcing or inspiring or enticing children to **not think** of shooting. Ever. Which means no feelings of revenge, whatsoever."

"How you do that?" Martha asked.

"I think the problem is too big to have only one solution. We have to consider multiple angles," Eugene said.

"What do you mean?" I asked, not wanting to be left out of the discussion.

"A recurring theme this, I know," said Eugene, "but we have to have mandatory mental health screenings and the preventive therapy we talked about earlier. In addition, we need to actively instill values such as hard work, kindness, helping each other etc. etc. – let's call this character building. We should do this and provide a good education, if not a great education, for all children, no matter their socioeconomic status."

"We have to create an educational system that brings out the best in children," Moira said. "We have to create a process in schools that is actually FUN for children."

"Exactly," said Eugene, smiling at us. "We have to get children so excited about learning that they forget to think about their marshmallow, which in this case is shooting or some other type of violence."

"Brilliant," Moira said. "You are a genius, especially for thinking about building character."

"Not my idea," said Eugene. "These concepts are out there in the real world. Our school does a lot of things right. But imagine if we started focusing on building values and developing character. Actively building it, not just passively as in encouraging children to read certain books, or having them say *Sorry* and shake hands over perceived insults."

"School is the time to engage your mind in activities that will prepare you for adulthood. Get you to become really curious about how things work. I really like the idea of actively focusing on character," said Moira, jumping up and starting to pace.

"I think rich kids have a chance at all that." I didn't realize I had said that out loud until everyone had stopped talking and was looking at me to elaborate on that statement.

"Well, look at our public schools, for instance," I said, defensively.

There was silence as everyone, I think, remembered my conversation with Andy.

"What? Is it so horrible that I used to be in a public school?" I asked peevishly.

That got everyone talking again. At the same time.

Dan finally got through the noise with his question, "How bad was it?"

"The worst, most dismal years of my life. Talk about the opposite of building character," I said.

"Well, there you go," said Eugene, sitting next to me.

He patted my back and said, "Some schools have become day care centers. They go through the motion of classes, but there is no pride in a teacher's job. There are no goals for what a child might learn or goals for the future of graduating students. ALL schools should have these goals in place and not just the rich schools."

"If we add fun to the classroom," I said slowly, "I don't think I would mind staying past 2:00 or 2:30 PM every school day."

"I love that thought, Wayne," Moira said. "If we make our school days go to 4:00 or 5:00 PM and teach all children how to control their anger, how to develop empathy and kindness, teach them nutrition, and also take them through the preventive therapy you were talking about, Wayne, I think we would create an entire generation that would believe in the principle of being the best and helping others be the best, too. Imagine if we all did that?!"

"It has to start with a really good education for all children, no matter which school they go to," I said.

"I agree," Eugene said. "It's simple math. Let's say, right now we are fully engaging the minds of 500,000 children across the nation. And 10,000 of those children go on to do great things for the world. The other ten million children..."

"Why ten million?" I asked.

"It's a random number, Wayne. Let me finish," Eugene said with a smile.

"Sorry," I said, quickly.

Eugene continued, "If we disregard the other ten million children and they don't get a great education, then we are missing out on digging out the diamonds from that mine.

Simple Math. If 500,000 fully engaged minds can give us 10,000 gems, imagine what we could do if we gave ten million children the same kind of education?!"

"That will never work," Moira said.

"Why ever not?" Eugene asked, sounding surprised.

"Simple human emotion," said Moira confidently. "It's the same reason why people hate immigrants or some country club members hate newcomers or new money. People want to hang on to what they feel is theirs. I worked hard and made money so my children can have a better life. Why should those other children have it just as good?"

"But children don't ask to be born," said Amanda, sounding and looking bewildered.

"Amanda, I'm not saying I agree with that kind of loser mentality. I'm just saying why things won't work," said Moira, her voice raised, just a little.

"You know, it is really important that we not exclude poor children from a good education, if not a great one. I will tell you why," Eugene said, leaning forward, "The selfless reason is, education can lift people out of poverty. Why wouldn't we give everyone that opportunity? The selfish reason is, it makes society better. Imagine if every child everywhere on the planet got a great education and great mental health services. Can you see that is exactly the future we need to create?"

"I would like nothing better. But it all boils down to money," said Moira, shaking her head. "Who's paying?"

"Hold that thought, Moira," Eugene said. "We cannot provide a great education without great teachers. You realize that, right? So, we need even more money. Money to train teachers really well. Money to pay teachers really well."

"I agree with you," I said, looking at Eugene. Smiling at Mom, I said, "I know it was hard for me to focus on anything when we were poor. I was busy worrying about what could get worse. We really don't want our teachers to worry about money instead of focusing on us, right?"

"Can't we get all the billionaires to contribute?" Amanda asked, sounding very tired and very sad.

"How? What's in it for them?" Dan asked.

"Well, we have a new situation that didn't exist before, right? Everyone says school shootings are a modern phenomenon and that they are here to stay. Unless...." Moira seemed lost in thought.

"Unless what, Moira?" I asked him.

Moira looked up and said, "Unless our generation creates a unified front. Unless our generation demands changes. Unless we absolutely refuse to do anything expected of us **until** the decision makers step up and do what we expect of them. And let's think a little about these decision makers."

"Exactly," said Eugene. "Who put them in office?"

"That's a great question, Eugene. We also need to ask if our decision makers are doing a great job?! Not decent, not good, we want great." Taking a break from her pacing and sitting down again, Moira continued, "All of us have to make sure to vote as soon as we reach voting age. Let's have a voice so we are heard. Let's unite so at the very least we can ask them to..."

I completed Moira's sentence, "Protect all children."

"Brava," Martha said, clapping her hands loudly.

"And" Moira said, "give all children a good education. Better yet, give all children a great education."

Martha clapped again.

"I like this very much," Eugene said happily. "To recap, there needs to be mandatory mental health screenings."

"Wait," Mom said. "I've been thinking about this a lot. I think we will run into a lot of problems if we mandate mental health screening. A baby step would be to train all parents and professionals who interact with children to recognize mental illness. Once that initial suspicion is stirred, then we can proceed to the next baby step, which is to provide recommendations of services."

Eugene said gently, "That's too mild, my love. Too passive. We have a new paradigm and we need new solutions."

Mom grimaced and said, "I sort of agree with you, honey. But I really don't think mandated mental health screenings are going to work."

"All the money that would go into training teachers to use firearms, we can use those funds to hire mental health professionals for schools," said Eugene. "That is the solution. We need to detect mental illness in various settings, at homes and in schools. But we also need to put in place the therapy sessions for all children, regardless of diagnosis – our preventive therapy sessions."

"Perfect," Martha said. "I don't like idea of training teachers to carry weapons like cops. Cops go to police academy. Not easy program. Is competitive and intense. How we can ask school teachers to be like cops but without police academy training?"

"What about the marshmallow?" I asked.

"We definitely need to distract the would-be shooters from focusing on the marshmallow," Moira said, standing up and starting to pace again.

"And here we come to the gazillion dollar question," Amanda said. "How?"

"What about parents?" Martha asked.

"What do you mean?" Amanda asked, frowning a little.

"You make effort inside school to diagnose and treat mental illness. That great. But how we train parents so they recognize mental illness in children, when very young! How parents can seek help for children soon rather than later?" Martha asked.

"That's what I want to know too," Mom said. "We have to train all parents to recognize signs of mental illness."

"Maybe the same professionals hired by the schools can teach parents. Maybe employers can give their employees free classes in recognizing signs of mental illness," Eugene said.

"Great ideas," Martha said. "One more thing. It not enough to diagnose mental illness. Doctor has to train patients and parents about warning sign if medicine not working. Explain why treatment, it is important. In my country, neighbors support each other in everything. And that feel so good. Good, kind people make you feel good mentally. Here in America, we need support groups for mental illness."

Moira said, "I love it, Martha. But I have a suggestion. I think we should have support groups for mental health or better yet, mental wellness. Doesn't that sound much better?"

"Good one," Martha said, finally breaking out into a smile. "I finish cooking now. Lunch ready soon."

"What about alternate therapies?" Moira asked.

Eugene asked, "What about them?"

"Our friend Maisy can afford to get psychomotor therapy to overcome trauma because her parents are wealthy enough to have a brilliant psychiatrist come to their home and offer this treatment that is not paid by insurance. But what if a poor child can benefit from this, but does not have access to it because he cannot afford it?" Moira asked.

"But Moira, we are talking about mental illness, not recovery from trauma," Dan said gently.

Moira laughed angrily and said, "And do you think the two are not connected? Yes, a school shooting is a traumatic event and can leave you with PTSD. But also traumatic is domestic abuse, along with sexual abuse, accidents, and growing up in violent neighborhoods while witnessing murders and drive-by shootings. What are the solutions to those events? Believe me, I felt so much rage after the school shooting that if I had acted out, I would have been labeled mentally ill. Couldn't any child who has gone through those other kinds of trauma potentially feel rage and helplessness? And if we don't resolve that inner conflict, how far will it go? Who is responsible?"

When Moira fell silent, I asked, "What about medication?"

"Our dad says medications alone don't often deal with the underlying issues, Wayne," Moira said quickly. "To get to a long-term solution, we have to deal with the underlying issue. Rearrange our thoughts. Create new virtual memories. Trick the brain into rewiring new thoughts. And that's where, I think, your Internal Family Systems therapy and psychomotor therapy are so helpful. But we have to make sure insurance can make these therapies affordable."

"Sounds like we have to speak to our representatives and our senators about this. Tell them what we, the people, want and need." Eugene said with a laugh. "Tell them to make mental health services affordable for everyone."

"Wait, one more thing," I said, quickly. "We never talked about all those places that sell guns to mentally ill people."

"Good point, Wayne," said Eugene. "It's a complicated issue. Although there are federal laws that prohibit sales of firearms or ammunition to mentally ill individuals, that law is only for people who were involuntarily admitted to a mental institution. In Florida, our laws also ban sales to people who have voluntarily committed themselves to mental institutions."

"Sounds easy enough, honey," Mom said.

Eugene shook his head and said, "It's complicated because not all licensed firearms dealers conduct background checks to screen out mentally ill people. And even if they conducted background checks, the dealers don't always submit their results to the FBI. This means if a licensed dealer in a different state looks in the FBI database for anything that prohibits sale of a firearm to a certain person, they are not going to find anything – simply because previous background check results were never submitted."

"Oh, this is not good," Moira said loudly. "I'm sorry to interrupt you, but I just googled this issue, and apparently, you can bypass all these background checks and just purchase firearms online."

"And that adds to the complexity of trying to keep guns away from the wrong hands," said Eugene. "It is not illegal to sell privately without running a background check. We need laws that will make all sales of all firearms and ammunition contingent upon passing a background check."

Something had bothered me during this give and take between Eugene and Moira. I raised my hand and said slowly, "Are we only talking about not selling firearms or ammunition to people who either voluntarily or involuntarily stayed at a mental institution?"

Eugene said, "Yes, we are, son."

I scratched my head, because I felt the answer was so simple and couldn't believe it was overlooked. I said, "How about we sell guns only to people who show that they've passed a test for mental illness?"

"How far back does that test have to go? One year?" Moira asked.

"Maybe the mental health professionals can tell us how far back the test needs to go," Eugene said.

"What if they show us forged certificates or somehow force their doctor to give them a clean bill of health? And what about all those guns on the black market?" Mom asked. "How will we ever trace the seller? Who will force them to obey this new law of asking for a doctor's certificate?"

"That's why we need multiple solutions," Eugene said excitedly. "We push for a new law that will ask for a clean bill of mental health for anyone who wants to purchase a gun. And this mental health certificate should come from a psychiatrist or psychologist, who needs to be above coercion of any kind. And we have to have all those other measures we talked about, including great schools, insurance coverage for mental health, preventive psychological therapies, good education and character development for all children, mental wellness support groups, and neighborhoods where neighbors genuinely care for one another."

I had a sudden flash of one of my favorite excerpts from 'Tuesdays with Morrie – *Do I wither up and disappear or do I make the best of my time left?*

"I will do it," I said, jumping up from my seat on the sofa. "I know now why you were asking me to give interviews earlier, Moira. This is my window of time to be heard. I can reach everyone, especially other children."

"What will you say?" Amanda asked, looking excited.

"I will ask every child who goes to middle school and up, to call or email their Representatives and Senators and ask for everything we've been talking about. This needs to happen immediately. We have to stop the hate, right away."

Moira raised a finger and said, "And all caring adults need to join in. We need as many people as we can."

"We need the President on our side to hasten things along," Mom added softly.

"I will see what I can do," I said with a smile.

REQUEST TO YOU

I am grateful to YOU, the reader for choosing to read this book. There are so many wonderful reads out there and I am sincerely grateful to have you read this one.

I would love to hear from you. Please leave your reviews, comments, and suggestions on
- goodreads.com (search for Bindu Mayi and click on the book, 'Something has to change')
- amazon.com (log into your amazon count, search for Bindu Mayi and click on the book, 'Something has to change').

I have a few requests, please:
- recommend this book to others if you have enjoyed reading it
- talk to your schools, churches, temples, youth groups, etc., about how the community can prevent shootings in the future
- have an opinion and express it in a respectful manner
- call and email your representatives and senators about (1) creating a law that makes it mandatory for buyers of guns, rifles, etc. to have a recent clean bill of mental health from a psychiatrist or psychologist, and (2) to require insurance companies to pay for mental health screenings and therapy.

ACKNOWLEDGMENTS

Thank YOU for reading this book.

My sincere gratitude to my husband, Sachin Mayi, for his constant support and encouragement, and to our families for their love and support.

Thank you to these wonderful folks for being my pre-print readers and giving me feedback: Rei Barbas, Yvonne McAlpin, Sachin Mayi, Dr. Madhavee Buddhikhot, Catherine Fitzpatrick, Raven Wallace-Ross, Dr. Robert Speth, Aditi Nair, Dr. Luigi Cubeddu, Dr. Scott Poland, Dr. Nicole Cook, Judy Dempsey, and Dr. Adele Besner.
Thank you, Dr. Poland for your kind testimonial.
Thank you, Gen Venckauskas and Yvonne McAlpin, for letting me interview you regarding school drills, class periods, school life, et cetera.

I have drawn inspiration from reading 'Anne Frank The Diary of a Young Girl' as well as 'Tuesdays with Morrie'. I have also been tremendously inspired by Dr. Bessel Van Der Kolk's book, 'The Body Keeps The Score' – which introduced me to several forms of effective therapies. I highly recommend this book. I also recommend reading Malcolm Gladwell's article called 'Thresholds of Violence' featured in the October 19, 2015 issue of the New Yorker.

The cover design was by Bindu Mayi. Art by Emana Sheikh. Thank you, Emana. The cover was created by Aditya Nair. Thank you, Aditya.

ABOUT THE AUTHOR

Bindu Mayi has a doctorate in Molecular Microbiology & Immunology. She currently teaches Microbiology to health professions students at a University in South Florida. She is also a Board member and volunteer for Share-A-Pet, a 501c3 nonprofit organization that provides free pet-assisted therapy to individuals in hospitals, nursing homes and children's centers. Visit www.shareapet.org to learn more about making your dog a therapy dog.

This is Bindu Mayi's second book.

You can first read about Wayne Benko in her previous book, 'Mrs. A', which features the origins of Wayne's MRSA infection as well as Andy's transformation from zero to hero.

Both books are available on Amazon (search for Bindu Mayi).

NOTE FROM THE AUTHOR

My family and I have been deeply saddened by the many school shootings in the United States. The one closest to our home was the one at Marjory Stoneman Douglas (MSD). My husband's nonprofit organization, Share-A-Pet, sent therapy dogs to MSD in the immediate aftermath of the school shooting. We have been in awe of the tremendous energy, eloquence and clarity shown by school children from MSD, as well as inspired by their ability to get their voices heard.

When I started writing Wayne's story, I already had an established persona as a framework for developing the plot – of Wayne being a bully, which is more fully expressed in my first book, 'Mrs. A'. It is my belief that most people don't mean to be mean. I wanted to use that philosophy in creating a story about Wayne – one that doesn't paint him in shades of darkness alone, but also redeems him with shades of lightness. Once I thought of that, there was no question in mind as to how his story would unfold. I have loved writing this story and hope that you, the reader, find it compelling and thought-provoking enough to initiate a conversation with those around you. I don't presume to have all the solutions. But, I hope you are inspired to create a call to action – we need to remove the stigma associated with mental illness. We need to make mental health screenings routine and mental illness seen as something that can be managed.

Children are a precious and irreplaceable investment in the future of the human race. It is our responsibility as adults to provide a safe and nourishing environment where children can get educated, learn by example, be unafraid as they soar to great heights of their potential, and be inspired by visions of a world that is inclusive of everyone, irrespective of race, color, religion, appearance, and many other things, great and small, including mental health status. All of us, regardless of whether we are pro-guns or anti-guns want our children to be safe, and to receive a good, if not great education, and to fulfill their potential. We have to come together and ask coherently for this to happen.

It is my sincere hope that 'SOMETHING HAS TO CHANGE' will generate an earnest dialog and set in motion a process that gets us all moving towards easy and simple solutions.

Made in the USA
Monee, IL
06 August 2020